Something else

Virginia Fassnidge's first novel, *Finding out*, showed a rare talent and was widely acclaimed. This second novel amply fulfils that initial promise.

Amanda has recently lost her father and finds life without purpose. But his obituary notice attracts the attention of Gerald, a seedy antique dealer, whose unmarried mother once hinted to him the real identity of his father. Gerald sees this as an opportunity to introduce himself to Amanda, but his motives are dubious. The friendship that springs from that meeting takes him by surprise. Denny, Gerald's friend who lodges with him at his junk shop, is unnerved by this development, and himself embarks upon an uncomfortable, clandestine friendship with Amanda, in order to allay his jealous feelings towards Gerald's. Each friendship is separate, secretive and exclusive, but none can remain static. And tensions mount as deceptions are revealed, until events veer out of control.

Virginia Fassnidge has written a very subtle, ironic novel about the nature of friendship, in a voice that is uniquely her own.

By the same author

Finding out (1979)

Something else

a novel by
Virginia Fassnidge

Constable London

First published in Great Britain 1981
by Constable and Company Limited
10 Orange Street London WC2H 7EG

ISBN 0 09 464340 7
Set in Baskerville 10 pt by
Computacomp (UK) Ltd, Fort William
Printed in Great Britain by
Mansell (Bookbinders) Ltd
Witham, Essex

For Sidney, with love

1

Amanda woke, as she had on every morning of the weeks since her father's death, to a feeling of total hopelessness and loss which made the thought of opening her eyes unbearable, knowing as she did that they would be greeted by the mocking bright light of summer that found cracks between the heavy velvet curtains no matter how carefully she had drawn them the night before. She tugged the blankets round her and pressed her face into the darkness of the pillow, so hard that she could barely breathe.

They say that you can't suffocate yourself, she thought, *apparently once your conscious self blacks out, your body is taken over by automatic processes that haul it back into life, whether you want to live or not.* … Something of the kind seemed to happen to her now, because it was not any effort of her will but a habitual force that made her roll over, throw back the blankets, and slide out of bed, almost in one movement, so that by the time her eyes opened she was already moving on the conveyor-belt of another meaningless and empty day. She washed and dressed, or rather her body did these things, like a brisk professional stranger, like a machine.

In the kitchen she took out food and ate it, made tea and drank it. Habit again. *I don't need this*, she thought, chewing and hardly tasting. *I could just stop. They say that after a little you don't even feel hungry. Your head gets light, you drift … that wouldn't be bad, drifting. But* (aghast) *already there's too much time, how can I fill all that time if I don't wash, eat, brush my hair, put my clothes on and take them off again?* She saw the grey monolithic days stretching out in front of her, never-ending.

At first there had been numbing shock and then wild grief; she had been wakened in the middle of the night by the sound and the tremor of her own violent weeping. There had, then, been things to do, and people to see: the necessities of the situation had forced her into a kind of brittle busyness. She had written letters to people whom she knew scarcely or not at all: over and over again the same phrases whose meaning had gradually dripped out of them, leaving only hollow husks. The funeral had ritualised grief. Slow sonorous music, wreaths that made living flowers seem artificial, cards with words that you never see anywhere else: *condolences*, *bereavement*, words still delicately filmed with dust from the attics where they have been stored away out of sight. She had smiled at faces and seen mouths move: those words again. …

She had worn a grey dress that day; she remembered looking in the mirror and seeing how the colourlessness of the dress was matched by the rest of her: her hair, her face, all drained of light. It was as though she saw herself through a haze of fine pale ashes.

People had been kind; she could not say they had not been. She could imagine them telling each other: 'Poor Amanda, we must do something …' and they had asked her to tea, to dinner, for weekends in the country. She had not gone. There was no one that was more than an acquaintance; she felt close to none of them. There was no one in whose company she could have given way, and she could not trust herself not to give way. Before long, the invitations stopped. People had other things to think about.

Of all the people whom she had to do with, Amanda found the solicitor least trying. He might well have felt sympathy for her but he made no effort to express it, since this was not at the moment his concern. The important thing for him was to explain to Amanda just how her father's affairs now stood and how they were to be managed in the future. She listened, and signed papers. Her father had left her no duties or responsibilities; only a place to live and money coming regularly so that she would never be troubled with the need to earn her own living. She thought that if she had been given the choice she would have preferred it to be the other way around. She would have liked involvement; even more, she would have liked to know that her father had considered her fit to be involved. It hurt her to think that he had effectively cut her off from all that had been interesting in his life.

It wouldn't have been like this for him, she thought, if I had been the one that died. There was so much else in his life apart from me; so little in mine apart from him.

The solicitor suggested that she should make her own will 'as a matter of form'. There seemed to her no point. 'There isn't anyone,' she said, blankly. He did not press her. 'Just something to bear in mind,' he said. 'Anyway I'm always here. If you need advice or. ...' It was then that she thought she could detect sympathy in him; but he kept it concealed in his brisk business manner, and stowed it with papers in his briefcase.

Amanda washed the few things that she had used for her breakfast and tried not to think of the hours which remained before she could sleep again. For all her thoughts of suffocation and starvation, she knew that she was cowardly and so condemned to life. If there had ever been a time for violence it had passed.

The telephone began to ring. *I don't have to answer it*, she told herself, but – habit again, or was it hope still moving feebly about somewhere? – she was already, as she thought this, walking into the living room, towards the shrill summons.

2

'I think the time is right,' said Gerald, buttering toast more lavishly than usual, in celebration of his decision. 'I think today's the day.'

'What for?' asked Denny, though he knew perfectly well; and Gerald, knowing that he knew, merely smiled.

'Well, why today, then?' Denny went on. 'Why not yesterday?'

'I have a feeling,' said Gerald. 'I think it's been long enough.'

'You could have done it last week, in that case. You could have done it any time.'

'Last week it wasn't long enough.'

'How can you possibly tell?'

'It's just a feeling, like I said. It's in the air. Give me the paper, let's see what my horoscope says.'

Denny pushed the paper across the table. 'You've got tea all over it,' said Gerald, disapproving. He found the page, read silently, laughed. 'What did I tell you?'

'What's it say, then?'

'*News of a relative may surprise you,*' Gerald read aloud.

'It isn't you', Denny objected, 'that's going to be surprised'.

Gerald ignored this. '*Financially*, it says, *this could be a good day.*'

'There you go.'

'Well, that's what it says.'

'Those things are strictly rubbish, anyway.'

'Well of course they are. All the same, it's funny, isn't it?'

'If you're serious you should do the *I Ching*.'

'No thank you. At least you can understand the things they put in here.'

'A lot of use if it's rubbish.'

'You really think there's something in that stuff?'

'You can't tell the future,' said Denny in the patiently exasperated tone of someone who's said it all before and hardly expects to be listened to by now. 'All you can tell is how you feel about a situation, so you know how to act. That's what the *I Ching* does, helps you discover what you feel.'

'I don't *need* the *I Ching* to tell me what I feel. I feel it's today. I woke up knowing it was today.'

Denny poured himself another cup of tea, dark brown and thick with leaves from the bottom of the pot, and put the spoon he used to stir with back into the sugar bowl. This would have annoyed Gerald if he had seen it, but he was not looking; he was staring up at the ceiling, that relief-map of cracks and flaking plaster and brown stains. Denny did not think that he was seeing it, either; there was a distant and dreamy expression on his face that the state of the ceiling could not possibly have put there.

'Have you ever asked yourself,' Denny said abruptly, 'if it's the right thing to do?'

'The right thing?' Gerald sounded vaguely puzzled, as

though he did not quite understand the words. 'Well, of course I have. I've thought about it a lot. As you know.'

'That's not the same thing, necessarily,' said Denny. 'Thinking about it, and thinking if it's right. What about her? What will she make of it?'

'I have thought,' said Gerald. 'But I don't know till I see her, do I? I don't know what she's like.' He picked the paper up again and began to turn the pages, brushing off further discussion.

'Oh well,' said Denny. 'What does mine say?'

'What's that?'

'My horoscope, what's it say?'

'Rubbish, *you* said.'

'All the same.'

'It says,' Gerald turned back until he reached the right page, 'it says, *nothing at all is going to happen to you today.*'

'It doesn't say that.'

'It says, *if you really want to know why don't you do the I Ching.*'

'Let me have a look,' said Denny; Gerald in a teasing mood was a rare enough event to be unsettling. He reached impatiently for the paper across the table.

'No,' Gerald twitched it out of the way, 'this is what it really says: *things may not always be what they seem. You should think twice before making any final decisions.*'

'Boring. Why do I always get the boring ones?'

Gerald shrugged, and went back to reading the paper. Denny watched him for a bit. 'Aren't you going to do it then?' he said at last.

'Not yet,' said Gerald.

'When?'

'Why do you want to know? You're not really interested, are you?'

'I am interested. I just don't think you're going to do it, that's all.'

'You'll see.'

'What are you going to say?'

'To Amanda?' Gerald's voice savoured the name. He leaned back in his chair, considering. 'Well, I'll begin by saying how sorry I am about her father, and all that. And then I'll say about how he knew my mother –'

Denny exploded into laughter. 'Will you, though? How biblical.'

'Biblical?' Gerald was thrown. 'How's that?'

'Well, you know what that means in the Bible.'

'I didn't realise you were familiar with the Bible.'

'Everyone knows the dirty bits,' said Denny. '*Adam knew his wife*. ... We used to have fun with that in scripture lessons at school.'

'Well,' said Gerald, 'naturally I'm not going into that, not right away. ...'

'So?'

'So, what?'

'What else are you going to say? It'll be a short conversation if that's all –'

'I hadn't finished,' said Gerald. 'I'll say I'd like to see her.'

'And if she says piss off?'

Gerald shook his head. 'She won't.'

'She might not use those words precisely. But if she –'

'No. She'll see me. I told you, I've got a feeling about all this.'

'It must be wonderful,' said Denny, with exaggerated admiration, 'to be so certain about things. I don't know how you do it.' Gerald might not have heard him; he was gathering scattered toast crumbs, placing them one by one on his plate with an air of great seriousness. 'Oh well,' said Denny, picking up the newspaper. He began to read, but his glance kept flicking upward, ready for Gerald to make a move.

Gerald sat in silence for several minutes, then, shaking himself slightly, like the hands of a clock jumping suddenly forward, he stood up, pushing his chair back.

'You going to ring her now, then?' said Denny, immediately alert.

'Yes.'

'These feelings of yours,' said Denny, 'do you hear voices? Little voices inside your head, saying *this is it, mate*?'

'Are you being funny?'

'No, I'm interested, that's all.'

'I don't hear voices,' said Gerald. 'I just know.' He started towards the door.

'Bet you she says piss off.'

Gerald left the room without replying. Denny turned to the horoscope page to see if Gerald had been making it all up: he hadn't. There was the sound of Gerald's voice from the next room, but it was too low for any words to be distinguishable. Someone somewhere had Radio One on full blast and the windows open, and someone else was yelling monotonous threats at children. Denny gave up trying to listen to Gerald. He picked cups and plates off the table and dumped them in the sink. The water heater went through its usual at-death's-door performance, groaning and gagging for half a minute before grudgingly releasing a thin stream of water. Gerald came back. He looked pleased with himself but said nothing.

'Well?' Denny, finally, had to ask.

'I was right,' said Gerald. 'Naturally I was right.'

'Naturally.'

'We're going to see her this afternoon.'

'Oh,' said Denny. 'What's this *we*?'

'I thought you'd come.'

'Don't see why,' said Denny. 'She's your sister, not mine.'

'I'd feel better if you did. You're good with people, when you want to be. I don't know what it is about you but you make them trust you. That's why old ladies let you cart away all the stuff out of their attics for a fiver and think you're doing them a good turn.' Denny laughed. 'No, it's true though, isn't it?'

'They don't trust you?'

'No,' said Gerald, aggrieved. 'They think I'm trying to pull a fast one.'

'You usually are.'

'Well, that's what it's all about, isn't it?'

'I don't think I want to come with you,' said Denny.

'The thing is', said Gerald, 'I'm nervous'.

'Never,' said Denny. 'You mean this feeling of yours isn't enough to give you complete confidence? You want your hand held?'

'Shut up,' said Gerald. 'Well of course I'm nervous. I don't know, do I?'

'What don't you know?'

'If she really is my sister.'

'I don't really see it matters,' said Denny. 'Long as you can convince her.'

'Well of course it matters!' said Gerald. He was amazed that Denny could think otherwise. 'Well, all right, then, don't come if you don't want to.'

'Oh, I'll come,' said Denny quickly. 'We'll have to shut early, though.'

'What's an hour or two? This is more important.'

'More profitable?'

'I didn't say that.'

'What you meant, though, isn't it?'

'No,' said Gerald. 'No, it isn't. You know it's not the money –'

'I believe you, thousands wouldn't,' said Denny. 'We ought to open up now, oughtn't we? It's late.'

'I don't expect they're queueing up outside,' said Gerald. The thought of the shop depressed him. He had no taste for the ordinary today; he wanted to be doing other, rarer things, and the hours between now and four o'clock hung on him like lumps of lead.

They went through to the shop. Denny unlocked the door and turned the sign round. Gerald looked briefly and with displeasure at the crammed furniture, the shelves piled with the unwanted contents of dozens of homes. The sunlight sliced through dusty air. Gerald's nostrils filled with the odour of other people's lives, sour and frowsty. He felt constricted here. 'I'm going out the back,' he said. 'I'll have a look through that stuff came in yesterday.'

'Rubbish, mostly,' said Denny.

'When isn't it?'

'What's she like?' asked Denny.

'Hard to tell over the phone, isn't it,' said Gerald evasively. He did not want to talk about Amanda any more just at the moment. He was beginning to regret now that he had asked

Denny to come with him; almost, that he had ever spoken of her at all.

'You must've got some impression,' Denny persisted.

'I don't know,' said Gerald. 'I can't remember'; though as he said this his ear could perfectly recapture Amanda's voice: clear, it had been, precise, cool? no, though it had held no warmth that was not the right word, but what is the word for a voice that sounds as though it knows it is speaking into emptiness and expects no reply?

3

'I don't think', said Amanda, 'he ever mentioned your mother,' then, hurriedly, afraid that she might have put it too bluntly to be polite – having been so much alone, she had grown unused to the niceties of conversation – 'I mean, he never did say very much about his younger days.'

'I don't expect he did,' said Gerald, reassuringly. 'My mother didn't say a lot, either.'

'I get the impression that he didn't have very happy memories of them, on the whole.'

'I know she didn't,' said Gerald. 'She did say that much.'

'He never went back there.'

'Not a place to go back to,' said Gerald. 'Nor did she.' He glanced round the room, appraising and approving. It was all just as he could have wished. Not ostentatious, but you could tell there was money there all right; everything breathed it, quietly and confidently. If he had been on his own, he would have touched things, rubbed folds of soft heavy curtain against his cheek, smoothed gleaming wood with his fingertips. 'Mind you,' he said, 'your father did all right for himself, didn't he?'

'Yes,' said Amanda. 'I suppose he did. Yes, he did. Of course.'

As for her ... Gerald thought. *I was right. The bottom's dropped out of her world. She'll need something, someone ... only, mustn't rush it.* He hadn't yet decided how he would do it. Or when. Not today, probably: too soon. Leave some opening, so he could call again. Not with Denny, next time. Denny was being a dead loss. Hadn't said a word so far. And had refused to change before they came. *Should've come on my own*, thought Gerald, and then, reminded by silence that it was his turn to speak, he said, 'My mother didn't. But then she wasn't the sort to do well anywhere, really.'

'No?' said Amanda, vaguely. She did not know what she could say, what she was expected to say to these people who had turned up so surprisingly; or rather to Gerald, who was doing all the talking – Denny, whose name she had forgotten and the explanation for whose presence, if there had been one, she could not now remember, remained silent, with an air of disassociating himself from the whole situation that made her all the more nervous. *It was a mistake*, she thought, *I shouldn't have agreed to this*. Only, that morning, when Gerald had rung, she had been startled enough to grasp what had seemed at the time like a momentary escape from her terrible monotonous despair. She had thought that, somehow, the necessity of getting together a kind of personality to present to strangers might be good for her. She had taken more care than usual about what she looked like, not out of vanity but simply because for the first time in weeks she needed to consider how she would appear to another person. It had not been much use though after all, since her inner self remained obstinately the same. She sat stiffly, her fingers twisting and pleating the folds of her skirt, and wished very much that they would go away and leave her alone. Her mind was numb.

They did not go. The silence swelled around them until she could no longer bear it, and in desperation she offered them tea. It seemed a normal thing to do, and she felt a great need for normality, and an occupation for her hands which were developing an obsessional life of their own, however much she tried to keep them still.

'That would be nice,' said Gerald, and she escaped, with relief, to the kitchen, closing the door behind her as though this might end their existence. She moved slowly as she filled the kettle, prepared a tray, partly to spin out the time, and partly because she found that her hands were shaking so much that she needed to be very careful. She poured milk into a jug and filled the sugar bowl, realising how long it had been since she had done things so elegantly.

As soon as she had gone, Gerald turned to Denny and said, in a low voice, 'I wish you'd say something. Just once in a while.'

'I wish I hadn't come,' said Denny.

'You could at least –'

'I didn't want to.'

'You didn't have to,' said Gerald.

'You asked me to.'

'Well, since you are here, though –'

'I don't like it.'

'I'm not asking you to like it,' said Gerald, impatiently. 'You don't have to look so bored, that's all.'

'Oh, I'm not bored,' said Denny.

'That's what it looks like.'

'Far from it,' said Denny. 'I don't think you should have come either.'

'She asked me.'

'You asked yourself.'

'She could have said no,' said Gerald. 'Why shouldn't I have come?'

'Oh, I don't know.'

'Come on,' said Gerald. 'You must've had some reason for saying that.'

'A feeling.'

'How do you mean?'

'A feeling. I get them too. She doesn't want us here, she's asking us to go away, all the time. Can't you tell?'

'She's making us a cup of tea,' said Gerald. 'That seems a funny way of asking someone to go.'

'She's had enough.'

'What of?'

'Us. We shouldn't be here. It's an intrusion.'

'Well,' said Gerald. 'Of course it's obvious she's had a bad time, I mean –'

'Is having.'

'All right. Is having. But all the same.'

'We're not helping. Can't you see?' said Denny. 'Can we go soon?'

'Look,' said Gerald. 'Isn't the worst thing, always, being alone?' Denny didn't answer. 'Isn't it?'

'Maybe.'

'You know it is.'

'It's a question,' said Denny, 'of when. And who, of course.'

'We won't stay long,' said Gerald. 'Not today. It wouldn't do to ... I mean, you're right in a way, I suppose. Only, just try a little, will you? Because you're not helping, you're definitely right about that.'

'I don't feel like saying anything.'

'Make an effort,' said Gerald. 'It wouldn't hurt you to.'

There was a rattling sound as Amanda, carrying the tray, opened the door. She came in a little more confidently than she had left. She could begin to see an end to this. They would drink the tea and then they would go, and leave her to her natural state. She set the tray down on the table with a feeling almost of triumph.

Denny caught something of this feeling; he had watched her closely since she had returned to the room. Gerald had been watching her too, but his attention was taken by the cups. 'Very nice,' he said, nodding towards them. 'Worcester?'

'Yes,' said Amanda.

Gerald was pleased because it had been a lucky guess. Amanda was pleased, too, that the conversation was turning to something external and easily defined. 'Yes, Worcester,' she repeated, wondering what else she could say, and touched the cup nearest to her, following the curve of its handle with her finger which she watched as though it were not her own, noticing the rough edge where earlier in the day the nail had split off. The sight depressed her immediately, as did always the signs of her physical disintegration that so accurately mirrored her mental state: the strands of hair that filled her brush or hung limp from her fingers when she ran her hand over her head, the pink froth from her gums that she spat into the basin when she cleaned her teeth. She lifted the teapot quickly; it was a distraction.

'There's only milk, I'm afraid,' she said. 'I hope you don't mind. Some people like lemon.'

'Milk's fine,' said Gerald.

'I don't have any lemons,' Amanda said. 'I'm sorry.'

'No, really,' said Gerald. 'I always have milk in tea.' He took the cup that Amanda gave him, drank, and said, 'Very nice.' Amanda smiled, a brief tic-like movement. 'A lovely cup of tea,' he went on. 'Don't you think, Denny?'

'What?' said Denny. 'Oh, yes,' in fact disliking its weak smoky taste.

Amanda held her cup firmly with both hands, not caring what they thought, or rather, caring but more concerned that she should not spill tea on her skirt and see them trying not to notice it. There was silence. Gerald drained his cup and accepted more. Denny, who had been making a pretence of drinking, refused.

While she had been waiting for the kettle to boil, Amanda had scraped the inside of her mind for sociable things to say, and now, finally alarmed by the oppressive quiet, said, in a voice that sounded to her far too loud and abrupt, 'What do you do?' She looked nowhere in particular as she spoke, but it was by now assumed by all three of them that Gerald would answer; which he did promptly.

'I've got a shop,' he said. 'We sell old things.'

'Antiques?' said Amanda, trying hard. 'Furniture?'

'Sort of,' said Gerald. He wished he could make it sound better than it was. 'Yes, furniture, bric-à-brac, you know …'

'Junk,' said Denny. 'Rubbish.'

'Of course,' said Gerald, who would rather Denny had continued silent, 'my aim ultimately is to specialise a little more.'

'Modern rubbish,' said Denny.

'I don't think I know what you mean,' said Amanda. She was disconcerted by Denny's sudden entrance into the conversation, and, unable to cope with attempting to relate to another person, turned slightly, but definitely, towards Gerald.

'What kind of things?'

'Well, the more modern stuff,' said Gerald. 'Old, but not really old.'

'Commemorative tea caddies,' said Denny helpfully. 'Guinness toucans. Jeyes Fluid bottles.'

'Really?' said Amanda, still to Gerald.

'There's quite an interest in that sort of thing,' said Gerald. 'You could have a really nice little shop. I know someone who specialises in tins.'

'Tins?' said Amanda.

'Boot polish tins, anchovy paste, anything. You know. All stuff that wasn't ever intended to be kept, but people appreciate it now. It's the design, partly. I mean, they are nice, some of them. And it's also the old nostalgia thing, that's very big now. It's the fashion, you know, it's like kids, one starts collecting bus tickets, they all collect bus tickets.'

'You could sell a collection of bus tickets,' said Denny.

'You can sell almost anything,' said Gerald. 'But there is a lot of rubbish all the same. You need an eye for it, you need to know what's likely to appeal. And of course you don't pick and choose when you're buying, you can't, that shows you're interested. You clear a house and try to get the people to think you're doing them a good turn, taking the stuff off their hands, but all the same you have to give some sort of price, and you'll get a lot of rubbish, real rubbish I mean, so that by the time you've got it all sorted out, picked out the good bits, you've already paid out a fair amount, you'll get it back of course, in the end, but meanwhile you have to live. So a lot of what we do at the moment is very ordinary stuff.'

'It sounds like very hard work,' ventured Amanda.

Gerald nodded. 'It's the only way though, isn't it? I mean you have to be prepared for that if you want to get anywhere.' He paused for a moment, then, 'Your father would have agreed with that, I should think.'

'Oh yes,' said Amanda, with a sudden warmth that was startling. 'Yes, absolutely. He always said it was no use waiting around for things to come to you, you had to go out and get them. He had such energy, he couldn't bear to be inactive, but it had to be useful activity, not just playing, things like golf, he didn't have any interest in that kind of thing.'

'Work was his pleasure, I expect,' said Gerald.

'Yes,' said Amanda, 'that's quite true. I don't think he really enjoyed anything else.'

'Well,' said Gerald, 'that's the way to do it.'

'What about your mother?' asked Denny.

Amanda turned towards him for the first time, staring at him confusedly as though the question touched on things outside her experience.

'I mean,' said Denny, setting his half-drunk cup of tea on the table, 'what did she think about all that?'

'I don't know,' said Amanda. 'I don't really remember what she thought. I was quite young when she died.'

'How old were you?' asked Denny. Gerald didn't think this was at all necessary.

'About fourteen,' said Amanda.

'That must have been very sad,' said Denny.

'I don't remember,' said Amanda. 'I don't remember her very well, really.'

Gerald cleared his throat, about to say something, but already Amanda was continuing, 'I don't think she appreciated him, I think she never understood him. She used to complain, she wanted him to work less hard, spend more time at home, she couldn't see that was how he was, how he needed to be.'

'Maybe he didn't need a home and family,' said Denny.

'Denny,' said Gerald.

'But there had to be something for him to come home to,' said Amanda. 'There wouldn't have been any point to it otherwise. You mustn't think he didn't care. That was what it was all for. He'd have done it all the same if he'd been on his own, because that was what he was like, but it was all to make something that would be different from what it was for him when he was young. She couldn't see that, but I knew that was what it was. And afterwards, all the time when it was just him and me, I tried to have everything the way he wanted it, to show him I understood, that I appreciated it. I know he really cared.'

With one part of her mind, Amanda was aware that she had started a descent into self-revelation that appalled her, but which she could no longer halt, and with horror she heard herself continue, 'Now I don't know what to do, there's nothing, I don't know how I can bear it.' She looked at Gerald, at Denny, as though they might be able to do what she could not do herself, stop this humiliating lack of control, and suddenly she began to cry as she had not done for weeks now, and never in front of other people. 'Please –' she said helplessly, though she didn't know what she was asking for, and Gerald turned on Denny a look that would have told him, *See what you've done*, if he had been watching Gerald instead of Amanda.

Gerald got up and crossed to where Amanda sat, tortured, her head twisted away from them, her eyelids cramped shut against tears. 'Amanda,' he said, 'you mustn't think you're alone.'

She seemed not to have heard him. He went on, unsure that he was doing the right thing, but unable to think what else he could do, now: 'Listen. I wasn't going to bring this up, not yet, anyway, but ... I never knew who my father was, she wouldn't tell me about him, or she'd make up stories and afterwards she'd say they weren't true, but she told me this, and she never went back on it, she swore it was true, and she said it was your father, Amanda, are you listening? That means I'm your brother, do you see, and you aren't alone.' He sat beside her, and after a moment's hesitation – it was not often that he voluntarily touched anyone – put his hand on hers.

Denny was watching, fascinated, saying inside his head to Gerald, *you're a bloody fool aren't you, she can't take it, what a mess you've made of it.* But Gerald had after all judged the moment rightly. Amanda, who throughout might not have been listening to him, she had remained so motionless, suddenly turned like someone aroused from deep sleep, and her wakening expression was of intense joy; she blazed with it. Denny, watching, found the change in her almost unbearable.

Gerald was taken aback. He had expected disbelief, demands for proof, questions at least; not the total acceptance with which Amanda so clearly received his words. In his surprise he made to pull his hand away, but she clutched it tightly in both of hers.

'It's only what she told me,' he said, confused. 'I don't really. ...'

There were still tears on Amanda's face, glistening; she had forgotten them. She stared at Gerald, and said in a dazed voice, 'You're like him, I hadn't noticed, I didn't look at you ... wait ...' She released his hand, and went quickly to the bureau. She searched in a drawer and came back with a handful of photographs. 'These are recent ones, it's not so obvious, but here, he would have been more your age then. ...' She used her fingers to mask off all but one figure. 'Don't you think? Can't you see yourself?'

Gerald had seen pictures of the man whose name his mother, after so many years, had finally given him: indistinct blurred newspaper photographs which he had studied avidly, looking for a resemblance and finding none. Now he saw staring up at him in glossy clear-defined black and white, not his own face, certainly, but something, all the same (he was not sure what) that he recognised, familiar and yet strange, as when you catch sight of your own reflection unknowingly and wonder briefly who that can be.

'I don't know,' he said at last, honestly, 'it's hard to tell'.

'And this one,' said Amanda eagerly, 'this is more like you still'.

Gerald stared, thrown off-balance by the unexpectedness of her working to convince him rather than the other way about. 'There is a likeness,' he said.

'Oh, there is!' she said, gathering the photographs together on her lap. She leaned back, exhausted by emotion. The shock of her loss had numbed her; this new shock, in its own way just as great, had opened her, she felt a sudden inrush of sensations, as though a vacuum inside her had been pierced. She smiled at Gerald, who returned her smile.

Denny said nothing. He felt that he should not have been there; at the same time, he would not have wanted to be anywhere else.

4

Gerald drove quickly, because he was restless, but carefully, since he needed to fill his mind which would otherwise have been spinning. He had not spoken since they left the flat. Neither had Denny. It seemed that each was waiting for the other to begin. It was Gerald who finally broke the silence. 'Well,' he said, inadequately, because there was no way of saying what he felt, 'that went off all right'.

'Oh yes,' agreed Denny. 'You could say that. I must say I thought you were making a mistake though at first.'

'You thought I was. Well I thought you were.'

'Me? What did I do?'

'You know. All that about her mother. Why did you want to go on like that for?'

'I was interested,' said Denny. 'Anyway you wanted me to talk to her.'

'Yes, talk, not start all that emotional stuff. That wasn't what I'd intended. Don't you see, I had to tell her then. She'd never have wanted to see me again, not after that.'

'She just needed to let go. Nothing to do with anything I said. Anyway, I don't see what you've got to complain of.'

'Well, yes,' said Gerald, 'as it happens it's all worked out quite well, that's the main thing.' After a little, and while making a great show of concentration on an overtaking manoeuvre, he asked, 'What did you think of her?'

'She's all right,' said Denny.

'Oh,' said Gerald, a little disappointed. 'You're in a bit of a funny mood, aren't you?'

'No I'm not. I've got a headache, is all.'

'It's a nice flat.'

'Very nice. You should have made her an offer for the contents.'

'I don't know what you mean.'

'Well, you did go on a bit. I thought that was something else you were going to leave till later.'

'Why are you being like this?' asked Gerald, hurt.

Denny could not, and in any case did not want to, explain how terribly he had been affected by Amanda's joyous acceptance of Gerald. 'I just think the whole thing's wrong, that's all.'

'How can it be wrong?' Gerald asked, amazed. 'You were on about that before. How *can* it be? You saw her. She needs me.'

'And you need her. Her money anyway. Fair exchange I suppose you think.'

'It isn't like that,' said Gerald.

'Come off it,' said Denny. 'You'd have bothered if she hadn't got money, you mean?'

'I probably wouldn't even have *known* about her –' Gerald began, and then stopped. There wasn't any need for him to justify himself. Denny could think what he liked. He didn't care, now. Anyway he wouldn't have found it easy to put into words the change in his feelings, not just since meeting Amanda, but before. What had started as a kind of game, a what-if exercise, developing into a possibility, had become, somehow, on the way no longer a fortune hunt (though that aspect of it did remain, there wasn't any use denying it) but the search for fulfilment of a need that he hadn't realised existed. He hadn't thought, he honestly had not thought, that he cared whether he knew who his father was or what he was like. Knowing his mother, he had wondered if perhaps it wasn't best not to know his father. And yet, once started, the whole business had taken an unexpected turn, and it was the finding of his sister, and not the financial benefits that might come of it, that now excited him and filled his mind. He couldn't expect Denny to understand all that. It was all very well for him to be censorious now, though, but he had taken his share in the what-iffing, when Gerald had first had the idea, constructing all kinds of impossible scenarios, involving blackmail, murder, all the trappings of a thriller. In fact Denny had been a good bit more imaginative, to start with; but he'd got bored with it before long, it seemed.

So Gerald didn't try to explain himself any further, but drove silently home. As soon as Denny got indoors, he filled up the kettle.

'What's that for?' asked Gerald.

'Tea,' said Denny.

'We just had some.'

'That was hours ago. Any rate it was lousy.'

'No it wasn't,' said Gerald.

'I couldn't drink it.'

'It was Earl Grey, I think,' said Gerald.

'So what,' said Denny.

'I feel like going out somewhere,' said Gerald.

'I don't.'

Gerald looked glumly round him, at the dingy kitchen, which seemed to him more than ever cramped and sordid. He kicked at the place beneath the table where the lino was cracked and curled up like a bit of stale bread. 'I mean outdoors,' he said. 'We could run up to Hampstead Heath or somewhere. It's a lovely day still.'

'Go on then,' said Denny. 'I've got a headache.'

'You need some fresh air then.'

Denny ignored him. 'Want a cup of tea?'

'No thanks,' said Gerald. 'Listen, I don't expect you to understand this because you couldn't care less about your family, but it really meant something to me, today, you know.'

'Oh yes?' said Denny, hardly listening at all, being too deeply involved with his own thoughts. Gerald watched him carry his mug of tea out of the kitchen, and presently the sound of the record-player, too much bass as usual, thudded down through the ceiling. Gerald poured himself a cup of tea after all but was too restless to sit down at the table; he walked about, feeling excited, elated, his aggravation at the sight of the four mean walls closing in on him continually dispersed by the boundless feeling welling up inside him. He looked outwardly calm, even sedate, his expression could have been that of someone worrying gently at a not especially important though intriguing thought, but inside, he did handsprings and leaped and watched rockets spilling stars across the sky.

After a while he went upstairs and banged hard on Denny's door, to make himself heard above the discordant music. 'How's your headache?' he shouted, looking round the door at Denny lying stretched out on his unmade bed.

'What's that?' said Denny, reaching out to turn down the volume.

'I said how's your headache.'

'It's all right.'

'Have an aspirin.'

'Can't be bothered. Not that sort of a headache anyway.' Denny stared unfocused at the ceiling and wished that Gerald would go away. Gerald looked at him and thought he really wasn't looking all that bright. He was sorry to have no one with whom to share his soaring mood.

'Well,' he said, 'I'm going out for a bit.'

'Okay,' said Denny, turning the music up and shutting his eyes. Gerald left, heading for grass and sky.

Denny lay perfectly still for a long time, moving only when the record finished. He switched off. He did not feel like noise, although he didn't really have a headache: that had just been an excuse because he couldn't take any more of Gerald in his present state. He was aware of Gerald's mood; he did not think that Gerald had guessed anything of his. How could Gerald know how he felt when he himself could hardly comprehend it. It was as if a great hole had been punched right through him, so cleanly that as yet he had no sensation of pain, only a vast emptiness and the hint of pain to come. He was utterly changed; it was a mortal wound.

5

'It's gold,' the woman said, angrily snapping the catch of her handbag.

'It's not, you know,' said Denny.

'It is. He said so.'

'He was wrong. If it was gold it'd be hallmarked.'

'What's that then?'

'Little marks on the inside. Look, there's nothing.'

'It could have worn off, worn smooth, couldn't it?' she asked, still hoping.

Denny shook his head and offered her a price, more than the ring was worth, probably, but he thought it would be nice to get rid of her. She looked at the ring with disgust. 'Sodding bastard,' she said, Denny thought not to him. He watched various thoughts move across her face as she stood undecided. At last she picked up the ring. 'I'm going to take it to that place in the High Street,' she said.

'Suit yourself,' said Denny.

'You might not be telling the truth. You might give me what you said and then sell it for fifty quid.'

'Oh yes,' said Denny. 'I do that all the time. That's why I drive round in a Rolls.'

'Funny,' she said. 'Or you could just be ignorant.' She snapped her mouth shut; and her handbag, with the ring inside it.

'Did you hear that?' Denny asked Gerald who came in from the back as the woman left the shop. 'Bloody stupid cow.'

'Yes?' said Gerald abstractedly.

'Thought I was trying to do her over that ring. She reckoned it was gold.'

'Was it?' said Gerald, not in the least interested.

'Out of a cracker I should think ... I thought you said I inspired confidence. Not in that one.'

'*Old* ladies, I said.'

'Christ,' said Denny. 'How old do they have to be to be old?'

'Older than that,' said Gerald. He wandered aimlessly round the shop, adjusting things on shelves. 'Well,' he said at last, 'I'm going out.'

When Denny said nothing, he added, 'I'm going to see Amanda.'

'Do you want me to come with you?' asked Denny, casually.

'There's no need. I mean, I was glad you came yesterday,

even if you weren't exactly sociable, but no, it's okay now.'

'I expect you'd rather be on your own,' said Denny. 'I expect you've got a lot to talk about.'

'That's right,' said Gerald. He was surprised that Denny had offered, after the funny way he'd been yesterday, both at Amanda's and afterwards. It occurred to him that Denny might be trying, in a roundabout way, to make up for it; of course he'd never apologise or anything. Gerald was touched. 'Yes, well,' he said. 'I'm off then.'

'See you,' said Denny. He wished he could work out whether he was glad or sorry not to be going. Since yesterday, he felt that nothing was in its accustomed place. Objects that he had seen so often that he no longer noticed them suddenly startled him, presenting themselves to him in new and yet worryingly familiar shapes. When he was by himself, as now, he experimented with the touch and smell and taste of things, to find if these had changed as well. Though change was perhaps not the right word, he thought, it was not change in the sense of things departing from themselves, rather they had become more truly themselves, their real shapes, colours, textures emerging from shadow. He'd had this kind of experience before but somehow it was different this time. He looked at a thin line of sunlight sliding in through a door that was not quite shut. Motes of dust made suddenly visible moved confusedly in it. Denny reached out so that the blade of light ran up his arm, whose pale hairs shone in it and cast tiny shadows. When he closed his eyes, but only then, he could feel the line of warmth where the sunlight fell. All this awareness hurt.

Unlike Gerald, he did not find inactivity irksome when he was in a highly charged emotional state. He would have preferred to sit immobile and watch the apparently random movements of dust-specks, but reluctantly he forced himself at last to go into the kitchen. There, he took from under the table a box of crockery that needed sorting and cleaning before it could be put in the shop. There were cobwebs and desiccated spiders over everything. He ran a bowl of warm water and squirted washing-up liquid into it. The bubbles on the water's surface flashed green and purple. Once he had begun the job he found it pleasant, in a way. He was glad to have no interruptions from the shop.

He decided that it was good he had not gone with Gerald. He didn't think it would be helpful to him to see Amanda again quite so soon. Better to wait till the excitement of discovery between her and Gerald had died down a bit. Those currents were confusing, and made him angry besides. If he could see her alone, better still. What he needed to do, though, soon, was to do the *I Ching*. He just hadn't worked out yet what questions to ask. (*What's happened to me?* was one he did not need to ask; he could answer it himself.) No problem though, the questions would come. In the end, he'd always found, they asked themselves.

6

'I found more photographs,' said Amanda. 'I've been looking at them all day.' She had spread them out in rows on a little round table by the window, as though she had been playing patience. Gerald glanced at the photographs, to please her, but in truth he found that he had very little curiosity about his father. He was far more interested in looking at Amanda. She hardly seemed the same person as yesterday. She reminded him of something he had read once, about split personalities, how their whole appearance could be altered, not by anything so crudely obvious as make-up or a change in hairstyle, simply by a shift of mental or emotional stance, that created a new individual. Something very like this had happened to Amanda.

He laughed. 'I thought I was meant to be selling you the idea, not the other way round.'

'Oh, I know you're sure. I just wanted you to see.' She swept the photographs into a pile. 'You wouldn't have come if you hadn't been sure.'

'I wasn't sure, though, not till I came.'

'But you are now?' His certainty was as important to her as

her own, Gerald could see. He nodded.

'I thought about it a lot before I came. Whether I ought to, and all that. If it was the right thing to do.'

'How could it not be?' she asked.

'Well ... you mightn't have liked it.'

'Oh ... you mean I might have been shocked?' She considered this, for the first time. 'Well, no, I mean, he wasn't very young when he married my mother, you'd expect him to have. ...' She hesitated. 'I'm sorry, though, if he didn't do anything to help your mother. I suppose he didn't? I mean, at that time there wasn't much he could have done, if he didn't want to marry her, but all the same –'

'I don't think it was like that,' said Gerald. 'Knowing her, I'm sure it wasn't.'

'What do you mean?'

Gerald paused a little before he answered. He did not feel ready to talk about his mother. He hoped that Amanda would share his disgust; but she did not know him yet and he was afraid of tainting himself in her eyes if he said too much. He tried to keep his voice and words dispassionate. 'She didn't keep in touch with people. I don't expect he knew she was pregnant. Anyway she wasn't his sort. She was always a loser and I bet he could spot them a mile off.'

'All the same –'

'All the same nothing. She was no use, not to herself, not to anyone. You couldn't help her, you know. She'd never let you. I tried, often enough. It was like she was determined to destroy herself. It took her a long time but she did it in the end.'

'What happened to her?'

'All sorts of things,' said Gerald. 'Nothing good. Oh, finally, you mean? Drink, mainly. I'd gone by then. I'd had all I could take. It was no way to live.'

'I am sorry,' said Amanda.

'No, it's me who should be sorry. I didn't come here to depress you.'

'You're not,' said Amanda. 'You can't believe how I felt this morning. It was like someone lighting a fire in your room while you're still asleep, you know? You wake up expecting it to be cold, and there's a warm glow. ... I put the piece of paper with your address beside my bed, so that if I woke up and thought it was only a dream, I'd be able to see it and know it was real.'

'And did you wake up thinking it was a dream?' asked Gerald.

'No. I told you. It was real all the time.'

Amanda picked up the pile of photographs, glancing at the top one and then at Gerald. 'Checking, are you?' he said jokingly; she shook her head and pushed the pile to one side, as though the pictures had ceased to have any importance for her. She had looked at them enough. She had been afraid that she might have deceived herself into seeing Gerald as her father restored to her: that had been her chief feeling yesterday, the reason for her violent joy in her recognition of him. After he had gone, and she had managed to think more clearly, she had felt a little ashamed and had begun to question her response to him. Although she had looked forward to seeing him again she had also been apprehensive. The minute he had walked through the door, though, she had seen, not the similarities that she had traced so eagerly, but the differences, and she had felt a new delight in his otherness, and a sense of freedom that was strange to her.

7

'You're late,' said Denny. He was sitting in the bleak light of the kitchen, doing nothing.

'I never said when I'd be back,' said Gerald, 'so how can I be late?'

'I mean, it is late. In absolute terms. I hope you've eaten.'

'Of course I've eaten.'

'What did you have, caviare?'

'Of course not,' said Gerald.

'How is she, then?'

'She's fine. Oh yes. She asked after you.'

'What did she say?'

'What do you mean, what did she say? She said, how is your friend, I'm sorry, I've forgotten his name. If you really want to know.'

'I made a big impression, that's obvious.'

'You're lucky she only forgot your *name*,' said Gerald, 'sitting like a dummy most of the time.'

'What are you going to do now?'

'Go to bed, I thought. Seeing as it is late.'

'No, I mean, about Amanda. With Amanda.'

'I don't see I have to do anything about her or with her, not like that. ... At the moment it's just seeing her, talking, you know. ...' He hesitated, wondering if he should mention it, then thought, why not. 'She is interested in the shop idea, though.'

'You got round to that fast,' said Denny.

Gerald knew he shouldn't have said anything about it. 'She brought the subject up herself if you want to know,' he said stiffly. 'She said she wished she had something to do. She said she always wanted to get involved in her father's work but he wasn't keen on that. She started to ask me about the shop, that's all. I didn't –'

'All right, all right,' said Denny.

Gerald wanted to say, *don't be like this, can't you see what a great thing this is for me?* but it was late and he was tired and there seemed no point to it; so he said nothing.

8

Gerald was on his way out again. To Amanda's, of course: where else did he ever go, these days?

'Isn't she going to come here at all?' asked Denny. 'Would that be slumming?'

'She isn't like that,' said Gerald. 'She'd like to come. Only,' he looked irritably round the kitchen, the ragged lino, the dark stippling of mould on the walls, the litter of cardboard boxes and overflows from the shop, and he was ashamed. 'I would like to do a bit to it first. It isn't that she would mind, I know, but I do.'

'It never bothered you before,' said Denny.

'It's always bothered me,' said Gerald. 'It's just there's never time.'

'There's even less time now with you off over there like a homing pigeon every day.'

'Do you mind?' asked Gerald.

'Why should I mind?' Denny shrugged; but Gerald felt, all the same, that he was being accused of something. Though it wasn't fair. He was doing as much work as he ever had, and asking no more of Denny. His time was his own; he could spend it with Amanda if he wanted to.

'I don't know why you should,' he said. 'You sounded like you did.'

'Oh, go away,' said Denny. 'Tell you what, I'll paint the kitchen while you're out, then you can ask her over.'

'You're joking.'

'Yes,' said Denny. 'Why don't you paint the kitchen and I'll go and see her.'

'Very funny,' said Gerald, and went out, which suited Denny because he had decided what he wanted to ask the *I Ching* and he didn't fancy doing it while Gerald was in the house; not that Gerald would bother him if he was up in his room, but somehow he felt the need for complete privacy. The knowledge that Gerald was around would be distracting, he thought.

He went upstairs, and took the *I Ching* from the bookshelf and from a drawer a little leather drawstring bag containing three half-crowns, which he kept for this purpose, feeling vaguely that their worthlessness as spending money increased their value as aids to divination. He focused his mind on the question. It was, *Ought I to see her?* He took out the coins, holding them loosely between his palms, listening to the quiet clucking sound they made as they rubbed against each other. When the coins had warmed to his own body temperature, he shook them briefly in his cupped hands and dropped them on to the carpet.

He did this six times, pausing in between to record the result of each throw by means of solid or broken lines according to the number of heads and tails thrown; so that he was left with a six-lined pattern, the hexagram. As he leafed through the book in search of the appropriate page he found himself wishing that he had not started this. Without knowing precisely what he dreaded he was afraid of what he might be told. *It's probably all rubbish anyway*, he tried to console himself in advance, but he had the uncomfortable feeling that it was not. When he reached the page he held his hand over it for a moment and turned his head so that he would not catch a glimpse of it before he was ready. *I really do want to know*, he told himself, and looked. Words hurled themselves at him: *great possession, progress, success … no error*. He made himself go back and read from the beginning, with care, propping his mind open to prevent it from becoming entangled with the first idea to enter. The more he read, however, the more the message shone out, simple and alarmingly clear; he realised that he had been hoping for something more obscure, a meaning to be traced through tortuous paths of imagery. He let his thoughts fall slowly like raindrops from an overhanging branch. Time after time they fell in the same place. Darkness settled around him and he remained sitting on the floor, motionless, feeling shaken, scared almost. The knife in his entrails that was the memory of Amanda was twisted, painfully, by the thought that soon he would have to do what he had half been wishing the *I Ching* would warn him off from: see her again, alone. When he heard Gerald come in, close on midnight, he kept quiet, as though asleep, though it was several hours before he could relax his mind and body enough to make the pretence true.

9

She did at least remember his name now; that was something, Denny thought, and if she sounded just a little surprised, well, that was to be expected: it was surprising, at least he himself found it so, now that he was actually there, after a week spent lying in wait for an opportunity to present itself; during which time he had pondered restlessly the meaning of what the *I Ching* had told him and felt apprehension touch him now and again with cold fingers. Gerald's visits to Amanda had prevented him from making any move; he had not been obliged to look further than the point he had arrived at this moment, thanks to Gerald's absence all day at a sale somewhere in Essex. Now, all of a sudden, he was here, with her, and at a loss, rather, for something to say; he had planned nothing, no explanations were to hand. He looked round the room, afraid to look at her. He felt a strange constriction in his chest, as though his heart had shrunk too small to allow his blood easy passage.

Amanda in fact remembered him better than she thought she had, now that he was here; her mind must have assimilated him without her being aware of it at the time. He had still the same slightly mutinous look about him, she thought, as though he was here against his will, but she did not find this as disconcerting as she had done previously.

She noticed his glance wander to the television, where mouths moved soundlessly, contorted with foolish smiles. She had for years been in the habit, when she was alone, of leaving the set on, but silent, sometimes for hours; she could not have stood incessant noise, but enjoyed occasional glimpses of colour and movement, meaningless and undemanding, as people enjoy the flicker of tropical fish in an aquarium. She had forgotten that the set was still on; she moved towards it.

'If you were watching something,' said Denny.

'No,' she said.

'I suppose it's company,' he said.

'In a way,' she said. 'Did Gerald ask you to come?'

'Gerald?' said Denny, as though uncertain who she meant. 'No.'

'I thought he might have, since he's away today.'

'Is he going to be coming later?'

'I don't know,' said Amanda. 'It depends.' She waited for him to tell her why he was here, but he said nothing. 'I was watching something just now,' she said, since it seemed necessary for one of them to speak, 'about birds. A children's programme. It was very interesting. About migration. It was amazing. I thought, how can they not be frightened, setting off like that, thousands of miles, to places they've never been before? Did you know the young birds don't travel with their parents? I thought the older ones would go with them to show them the way, but apparently they don't, they go at different times.'

'Animals don't frighten the way people do,' said Denny.

'But they are afraid, sometimes, aren't they? If a bird's caught indoors it panics, it keeps on throwing itself against the window.'

'That's just because they don't know there's anything there. They can't understand what they can't see. They're pretty stupid actually. They keep trying because they can't work things out. Migration doesn't frighten them, they're programmed for it. They don't have any imagination, they can't think about the future. It's like it's only people who're frightened of death, you know,' he said. 'I mean of the idea.'

'I suppose that's right.' For a moment she remembered how the screen had darkened with thousands of beating wings, carrying the birds to an unknown and unimagined destination. She would have preferred to think of them as courageous rather than stupid. 'I'm sorry,' she said. 'I should have offered you a drink. Or coffee, maybe?'

'I don't want anything,' said Denny.

'Are you sure? It's no trouble.'

'Not unless you do.'

'No. Though I would if you did, I suppose. How silly.'

'Just pretend I'm not here,' said Denny. 'I don't mean to put you out.'

'But you are here,' she said. 'How can I?'

He smiled at her, and said nothing. It seemed to her that there should be awkwardness in this situation and yet she felt none. 'Why does one always feel obliged to offer people cups of tea and things?' she said, struck for the first time by the absurdity of it.

'It's a convention.'

'I think it's more than that,' she said, pursuing the question in her mind. 'It's a kind of magic. A superstition. If you give people things they can't harm you. Something like that?'

'It wouldn't stop most people,' he said. 'But then I don't want to.'

'You don't what?' Amanda asked, puzzled.

'Want to harm you.'

'Well, of course not.'

Denny began to nibble at his thumb nail. It was so quiet in the room that she could hear the clicking his teeth made as they met; she found the noise irritating but did not feel she could well ask him to stop; and besides, she recognised in this the same need for occupation, however trivial, that made her wind strands of hair around her fingers, as she was doing now.

'We haven't got television,' said Denny at last; for something to say, it sounded like. 'Gerald reckons it's a waste of time.'

'He's probably right,' she said. 'Oh. I didn't realise you and Gerald lived together. I expect he said but I don't remember.'

'He might not have. He doesn't need to talk about me.' He paused. 'Mind you,' he said carefully, 'don't get me wrong. I just live there because I have to live somewhere. That's all.'

'Oh?' She did not understand at first what he meant, and then, realising, 'Goodness, I never thought –' She could feel that she was blushing and she was angry with herself because of it.

'That's all right then,' said Denny. 'Sorry. You might have. I thought it was best to get it clear.'

'You are quite close though, aren't you?' she said. 'I mean, you came with him, that first time. For moral support, he said.' It amused her to think of Gerald's having felt that need.

'That what he said? I suppose so.'

'I'm glad –' she began, but Denny interrupted her: 'Look, would you mind not telling him I was here?'

'Didn't he know you were coming?'

'No. Don't tell him.' His voice sounded already resigned to her refusal.

'I won't if you don't want me to,' she said. It did not at the moment occur to her to ask why, although afterwards she wondered why it had not.

'It's just,' he said, 'I don't know, he might not like it, that's all.'

'I don't think he'd mind,' she said.

'He feels kind of possessive about you.'

'Is that bad?' she asked. 'I feel like that about him, I suppose.'

'It isn't bad,' said Denny.

'You can't think,' she said, 'what it's been like, having no one, and then, suddenly, there's Gerald, I can't explain. ... And I think he feels the same; oh I know,' she added quickly, afraid, because of the bleak look on Denny's face, that somehow she had hurt his feelings, 'it's not been like that for him, but all the same –'

'I know it's special,' said Denny. 'You and Gerald.'

'I don't mind,' she said, 'I mean, how could I mind, that he has other things in his life, friends, I wouldn't want –'

'Well, that's all right then,' Denny said. 'I think I'll go now.' She was sure, then, that she had offended him; but at the door he turned back. 'Can I come again?'

'If you like.'

'Thank you.'

'Why, though?'

'Why?' The question seemed to startle him, as though he had never asked it of himself. 'I don't know. Do you need reasons?'

'No,' she said; but as the door closed behind him she thought she might have said yes. It was too late now. She went back into the living room and turned on the television. Two people were talking; they smiled a lot and nodded their heads at each other. One of them gesticulated wildly and the other laughed. She considered turning up the sound to find out what it was all about, but the faces seemed to have nothing behind them and she wondered if it would make much difference if she did.

10

It had cost Denny an effort to leave, like that, after so short a time; he could have stayed for ever, but he was afraid that Gerald might, after all, get back early and come on to Amanda's, and it wouldn't do to meet him there; and anyway, he told himself as he walked away, maybe that was enough for one day? He was amazed, still, at the readiness with which Amanda had agreed to say nothing to Gerald. He used the thought of their complicity as a salve for the hurt caused him by the warmth in her voice when she spoke of Gerald. He walked through decorous grey streets and leafy squares, not homewards, since he could not face that yet, and thought, *I couldn't have expected more, not this time, could I?* but he felt disappointment gnawing at him nonetheless.

He reached light, noise, and crowds, and continued to drift, solitary, borne on a different current from that which whirled everyone else along. He went into a pub and drank beer, not really wanting it. He thought that it was a long time since he had eaten and that he should be hungry but he could not feel that he was. The sandwiches and salads on the bar counter had an unreal look about them, as though paint and polystyrene had gone into their making, and what little appetite he had shrank to nothing at the sight of them. The pub was as dark as a dugout. Illuminated showcases on the walls displayed World War II relics, shellcases, a Mickey Mouse gas-mask, ration books. He felt sick. *Perhaps I've got an ulcer*, he thought, but without any real conviction. *It would be a lot simpler if it was something like that.*

It was too early to go home. Gerald might be there. *I expect she will tell him though, all the same, whatever she said, why shouldn't she?* He went into a cinema a little way down the road and sat with a glazed mind in front of a screen where limbs writhed improbably among tangled sheets. It didn't seem to mean a lot to him.

He had a headache by the time he reached home; real, this time, and the dull wound was still inside him. The lights were out. In the kitchen was a heap of boxes spilling over with the things that Gerald had brought back from the sale. Denny poked among them briefly without enthusiasm. There was a dirty plate, knife, fork and cup in the sink and cold tea in the pot. Gerald had been too tired to do more than unload the van and get himself some supper. Unless – but, checking, Denny saw that the van was out in the back. Gerald was home asleep. Not at Amanda's.

Denny went upstairs quietly. He lay in bed and tried to make himself fluid enough to slip out from the iron grip on his temples.

11

'Why does it always smell of cats in here, when we haven't got a cat?' said Gerald.

'Maybe they come in from outside and piss in here when we're not looking,' said Denny.

'Why would they do that?'

'I don't know.'

'You were out late last night,' said Gerald.

'Not really,' said Denny.

'Do anything special?'

'No,' said Denny. 'Went to the pictures.'

'What did you see?'

'It was called *Sex-starved Virgins* or something,' said Denny.

'One of those,' said Gerald, disapproving. 'I don't know why you bother.'

'You think I should stay home and live on my memories?'

'Well, it would be cheaper,' Gerald said primly.

Denny laughed. 'You're right there. Load of old rubbish, really. Talking of which, did you get anything good yesterday?'

'Not much,' said Gerald.

'You going to Amanda's, tonight?'

'I expect so, why?'

'Just wondered.'

Gerald began to unpack the cardboard boxes. 'You going to help with this?'

'All right,' said Denny. 'Anyway it isn't cats, it's fungus.'

'What is?'

'The smell. It's fungus.'

'Where's the fungus?'

'Under the sink. Under the floor too I expect. Everywhere probably.'

'What a dump,' said Gerald.

'Oh, it's all right.'

'No it isn't.'

'Roof doesn't leak.'

'Yet.'

'You don't get people crapping on the stairs either.'

'I know it isn't as bad as some of the places you've lived,' said Gerald.

'Palatial, compared, really,' said Denny.

'Or me, if it comes to that,' said Gerald. 'That isn't the point. The thing is, there are better places.'

'You're just hard to please,' said Denny.

'Well,' said Gerald. 'There has to be something better than this. Doesn't there?'

'Oh sure,' said Denny.

12

'Want to see something?' said Denny.

'What's that then?'

'Wait a bit.' Denny was looking forward to this. He wouldn't have been, if Amanda had told Gerald about his visit, but it was a week now and Gerald had said nothing, so she couldn't have told him. He could feel quite friendly towards Gerald, knowing he was one up on him, and he was glad, because it would have been a pity not to have anyone to share this with. He turned off the light, which you always needed in the kitchen after about six o'clock, summer or not, it was so overshadowed.

'What are you doing that for?' asked Gerald. 'If you want me to see.'

'It'll be better,' said Denny. He put the parcel that he was carrying down on the table, and began to unwrap layer after layer of newspaper. 'What do you reckon to that?' he said finally.

'Silver?' said Gerald.

'Yes,' Denny said impatiently, 'of course it is.'

Gerald turned the dish upside down and peered at the marks on the blackened surface. 'Have you had a look at these?'

'Not really. I wouldn't know, straight off, anyway, would you?'

'Need to look it up. Turn the light on would you.'

'Not yet,' said Denny. 'Just look at it. That's all you have to do, just look.'

'I see what you mean,' said Gerald. He wished he knew more about things like this.

'Isn't it beautiful?' said Denny, reaching out to touch it.

'Worth a bit.'

'That too, of course,' said Denny.

'Where did you get it?'

'Off an old girl in Dalston. I gave her twenty-five quid.'

'Twenty-five? She must be crazy. Or else it isn't as special as it looks.'

'Well, she probably is,' said Denny. 'It is special, all right.'

'Let's have another look.' Gerald hefted the dish in both hands as though he could learn something by doing so. 'Where would she get a thing like this?'

'Nicked it,' said Denny.

Gerald set it down carefully among the crumpled newspaper. He sat back and looked at Denny for a little without saying anything. At last, 'Do you mean that?'

'Yes.'

'How can we touch it then?'

'It's safe,' said Denny.

'But if you know she –'

'It's all right.'

'How can you be sure?'

'I'll tell you,' said Denny. He sat down opposite Gerald and began to trace the flower and fruit design on the rim of the dish lightly with one finger. 'If you think this is a dump you should see where this old lady lives. Horrible. She's ninety-three, can you imagine that? She can just about get around though I suppose one day she'll fall out of bed or something. However. During the war she was working in this big house, cleaning, very grand people, lots of nice things, only somehow they weren't very good at paying her wages, you know the sort, never any ready cash, would you mind frightfully waiting till next week, Mrs Thing. You know. So one day she got a bit pissed off, having to wait for her five bob or whatever they got those days. So she had a kind of brainstorm and walked off with the dish.'

'Yes,' said Gerald, 'but –'

'I haven't finished,' said Denny. 'So the next day she got cold feet and thought she'd take it back and no one would know anything about it. Only, this is the joke, when she got there, there wasn't any house.'

'How do you mean?'

'Direct hit during the night. No house, no people. All the stuff burnt or smashed or blown Christ knows where. So she went back home with the dish and wrapped it up in an old pair of knickers and put it in a cupboard.'

'She never tried to sell it?'

'Of course she didn't. Too bloody scared.'

'Why now, then?'

'I don't know, really,' said Denny. 'She felt like talking. I didn't mind listening. I didn't have anything better to do. She went on a bit, told me all sorts, then she told me about the dish. Asked if I wanted it. I think she was tired of having it around. Glad to have it off her conscience.'

'Twenty-five pounds,' said Gerald, wonderingly.

'Yes.'

'What do you think it's worth?'

'No idea,' said Denny. 'Lots. Anyway that isn't really the point.'

'I'd have thought it was.'

'Oh well,' said Denny, 'you would, wouldn't you?'

'I suppose, if it is silver,' said Gerald, 'even melted down, these days ... it'd be safer –'

'Oh no you don't,' said Denny.

'Well, it would be safer. There could be a record of it somewhere, you never know.'

'After forty years?'

'There might be.'

'I wish I hadn't showed it to you now.'

'Well, you have.'

'I paid for it.'

'What with?'

'I mean, let's take it I paid for it. I'll let you have the money. So it's mine.'

'You *didn't* pay for it though.'

'If you want to have it melted down I did.'

'All right, we'll risk it,' said Gerald. 'You're probably right, after all that time it's safe enough.' He held the dish on a level with his eyes. 'Do you think it's Georgian? I wish you'd turn the light on.'

'Leave it alone,' said Denny. 'It's not necessary. It's so obvious.' He tore a corner of newspaper and began to fold it, in two and then again and yet again. 'Do you know,' he said, 'you can't fold a piece of paper more than eight times? Doesn't matter how thin it is, you can't fold it any more than that.' He looked at Gerald. 'I'll tell you something, she really depressed me, that old lady. Mrs Tribe. Do you know, she's been on her own since 1943? Her husband was killed in the first war, she brought up the two kids, the son got his in the second, the daughter got married and went to Canada after the war.'

'You had quite a talk.'

'She sends a card at Christmas. The daughter. Doesn't write.'

'At least she sends a card,' said Gerald.

'Okay,' said Denny. 'But my brother and sister can look after the old ratbags. If they're still alive, that is. Of course they may not be, by this time.'

'Charming,' said Gerald.

'You can talk,' said Denny. 'As if you weren't relieved when your mother snuffed it.' Gerald made no answer to that. Denny went back to his paper folding, tearing off scraps with his thumbnail, and now and then glancing up at Gerald, who sat still, giving nothing away. At last, 'You know, when I was a kid,' said Denny, 'I thought I'd probably do myself in when I got to thirty, it didn't seem worth going on after that.' He shook the paper out and held it up, admiring the lacy pattern he had made. 'Pretty, isn't it?'

'You had a bloody good try,' said Gerald.

'I did, didn't I?' said Denny. 'Now I think I'll wait till forty, see what it's like and have another think. But ninety-three, yuk. Can you imagine it, think how long it's been since that old girl touched another human being?'

'There are other things,' said Gerald, revolted.

'I didn't mean that,' said Denny, 'though I don't know, they say you don't have to get past it, ever, don't they? I just mean touching. Contact. You know. That's why people keep pets, isn't it? Something to touch. Shall we get a cat? – Mrs Tribe hasn't got a cat. Or a dog or even a bloody budgie. I think people must just shrivel up inside, quietly, on their own.'

They sat in silence for a little, one each side of the table, with the silver dish between them. In the twilight it seemed to give out a faint glow. 'Well,' said Gerald. 'I'd better be off.'

'I won't ask where you're going,' said Denny. 'Give her my regards.'

'Yes,' said Gerald. 'You going out?'

Denny shook his head.

'You could give that a bit of a clean then.'

'I'm not touching it,' said Denny.

'It'd look better.'

'It looks lovely now,' said Denny. 'I'm not mucking about with it.'

'All right,' said Gerald. 'Put it somewhere safe.'

'Don't worry about it. Enjoy yourself. So long.'

'I haven't gone yet,' said Gerald.

'What's keeping you?'

'I don't know,' said Gerald. He stared at the dish, although that was not, particularly, what was on his mind, until Denny said, impatiently, 'Go on, clear off, I've got things to do.'

13

As he made his way across London, it seemed to Gerald that the depression Denny had spoken of earlier had somehow slid across the table and taken up with him instead. It was his passenger, sprawled lumpily in the seat beside him, forever edging nearer.

He didn't have to say that, Gerald thought. *He really didn't. It just shows, he's no idea. ... He ought to though, I've told him. Haven't I? All that talking ... but then that was him. I know about him. ...* Denny had felt the need to talk, when they first met, and Gerald had been content to listen and say little while Denny spewed out the curdled contents of his mind. Gerald knew more than he wanted to know, more, perhaps, than Denny might now want known; but what did Denny know, what had he ever tried to know, about Gerald? *Is it my fault? It does matter to me, what he thinks; but have things got to be said all the time? ... Of course what really should have happened*, Gerald told himself, surprised he should not have seen this clearly long ago, *Denny should have gone, once he'd got rid of all that on his mind. Once he was all right. It'd have been better* ... Only, there hadn't seemed any reason for him to go. Where to? And who would Gerald have found to do the work and be no trouble? There were never any arguments about money, hours, things like that. The arrangement suited both of them. But there was something that Gerald was finding irksome. *The thing is ...* The thing was, there was no room for growth in their relationship, it seemed. They were fixed now in attitudes and in perceptions of each other that were not likely to change. *It must be like being married*, he thought, and was faintly embarrassed to think in those terms, *only* … in marriage the possibility exists, at least, of breaking through the crust of habit that forms imperceptibly around a relationship, things happen, there are crises, emotions crack the surface, and people catch glimpses of their true selves. There's a chance. … Now that the time for confidence had passed, they were not likely to come to anything like that; though *it doesn't really matter now, of course, but still.* … Gerald could not help the strange feeling of regret at having, somehow, missed something. It was as though he realised (his love for Amanda thawing his congealed emotions) too late, that he might have loved Denny. There was no other word that he could find for it, although he was ashamed to use that one, even to himself, could never have expressed it so to anyone else. But what other word, finally, and how to say it without fear of being misunderstood? *Denny wouldn't understand, that's certain*, Gerald thought, *he doesn't know what it means, he doesn't understand about Amanda, about my mother* … he had not wanted to think about his mother any more, but there seemed to be no way of avoiding it. She had used men and despised them as they despised and used her, and the only person who was ready to love her without question she … Gerald forced his thoughts away; there was still too much pain.

There were times, he remembered shamefully, early on, when Denny had been laying the debris of his life out before Gerald, not asking for pity, not asking anything, when Gerald had been seized, briefly but violently, by an impulse to reach out his hand to him, and had (fortunately) been prevented from doing so by the knowledge that the gesture would have been, not rejected, but misunderstood, accepted wrongly. Denny would have been obliging; Gerald could imagine him saying (though not aloud): *this is what you're after, is it, why you let me go on so, why you listen so nicely, well okay then.* … But that hadn't been at all what Gerald had been after; what he wanted was what as a small child he'd cried himself to sleep with wanting: the warmth and consolation of belonging. Not that other thing, that not from anyone, ever.

These thoughts eddied in his mind as he climbed the stairs to Amanda's flat, and depression slouched close on his heels, not at all abashed at Amanda's shining welcome of him; it wrapped itself snugly about him as he sat in the twilit room, and Amanda, so eagerly observant, always, of him, could not help being aware of it, and asking what the matter was.

'Nothing, really,' said Gerald.

'It's as if you weren't quite here,' said Amanda. 'I don't mind,' she added quickly: she did not want Gerald to think that she was complaining. 'Only –'

'Just something Denny said upset me, that's all.'

'Denny?' said Amanda. She could only suppose that Denny had, after all, told Gerald about his visit, and that Gerald had not liked it, and liked even less the fact that she had said nothing about it; she felt, for the first time, guilty.

'Oh well,' said Gerald, 'you know Denny. I mean, you don't, of course. It wasn't anything much ... only, we were talking, just before I came away, he said something about how I was glad when my mother died.'

'That wasn't a very nice thing to say.'

'No,' said Gerald. 'The thing is, it's true, of course, in a way, but not like how he said it.'

'You were glad?'

'I thought I was. I mean, it seemed the best thing. It was as if, I don't know, it wouldn't matter any more –'

'Just because a person's not there –' she began.

'I *know*,' said Gerald. 'I know it doesn't work like that.'

'Why did it upset you so much, that he should say it?'

'I don't know,' said Gerald. 'I told you, it wasn't really anything, just, he was so casual about it. He doesn't understand.'

'What doesn't he understand?'

Gerald thought carefully before he spoke again. He wanted to make it clear to her; if she could not see, he felt, he would be lost. 'I've told you about her,' he said at last.

'Yes.'

'What she was like, what it was like, all the time. Till I couldn't take it any more. The drinking, and the men, and not knowing when she'd come in or what state she'd be in when she did. She left me on my own, you know, for three days once.

I was eight. I thought I'd never see her again. I thought she'd had an accident, been killed. Or just gone away. ...'

'That's terrible,' said Amanda. 'How could you manage?'

'There was food, it was all right. I was anyway pretty used to looking after myself. That wasn't important. It was just thinking she was gone for good.'

'If she had been,' said Amanda, 'at least you'd have been looked after better –'

'No!' said Gerald vehemently. Denny had said something very like that once; it missed the point. 'None of that mattered. I wouldn't have minded any of it, not those stinking places we lived, or what she did. Not much, anyway, only ... all the time, I loved her so much, and she never ...' he shifted in his seat, embarrassed by what he could hear himself saying, and glad of the half-light that concealed his face from Amanda. 'She never even touched me, not if she could help it. She'd push me away if I ... I'd have rather she'd hit me, I think, it would have meant something. Most of the time it was like she didn't care if I was there or not. And she was so unhappy.'

'She did keep you,' said Amanda, gathering up what comfort for him she could; 'she need not have. And she did come back, that time. Surely she –'

'No,' said Gerald. 'No. I have thought about that. I tried to tell myself she cared, really, just couldn't show it, but no. It wasn't that. She kept me because I was her excuse for having mucked things up. Can't you see? She could always say it was on account of me things had gone wrong. Not her fault at all. I went to see her once when she was ill, right at the end. I hadn't seen her for a couple of years, but I couldn't not go, not when she ... I thought maybe then ... but she was still blaming me. "I didn't have a chance," she said, "it'd have been different without you." I'd have done anything for her, Amanda, even then. But she wouldn't have it.'

In the gloom he could not make out her expression, and she did not speak; but presently he could tell, from the ragged sound of her breathing, that she was crying. She came and sat beside him; he felt her hand on his, and involuntarily moved away from her. 'Don't you like being touched,' she said, 'either?'

'I'm sorry. It's just I'm not used. ...' He surrendered his hand to her; her fingers tightened around it.

'I'm the one who should be sorry,' she said. 'You've had so little, and I. ... It's as if I've had what ought to have been yours.'

'It's not your fault.'

'If he'd stayed with her –'

'It wasn't like that, though, Amanda. I've told you. He never was with her, not the way you mean. And anyhow it wouldn't have made much difference, not to her. She never was any good. I suppose,' he added wryly, 'I suppose it's because I can say something like that Denny thinks I don't care. He doesn't understand. You understand, don't you?'

'Yes,' said Amanda. 'But have you told him? I mean, what you've told me. How you feel.'

'I don't know. Maybe not. It doesn't come easy, you know. Talking.'

'You can't really blame him then, can you?'

'I don't blame him,' said Gerald. 'I just wish ...' Amanda slid her fingers from his; he did not try to keep them. She got up and turned on a lamp. The soft confidential darkness crept away to the corners of the room.

'Do you like him?'

'Like him?' The question took Gerald by surprise. 'I don't know. Why?'

'I just wondered.'

'Well.' Gerald considered. 'It's not something you think about, is it? I suppose I do, yes. He's all right really. A bit funny sometimes.'

'How do you mean?'

'Moody. You know. Still it's not surprising. He's had a hard time. Used to be on drugs.'

'Did he?'

'Oh, yes. All sorts. He was well on the way to killing himself, I think, but he managed to get off it. You have to admire someone who can do that. My mother never could. I didn't know him when it was really bad, but he was still having to work at it, and it's not an easy thing.'

'It must have helped,' said Amanda, 'having you. A friend, I mean. Things are harder when you're on your own.'

'Aren't they,' agreed Gerald. 'Yes. He talked a lot, it seemed to help. He had a whole lot he needed to say. I suppose it did help. Only. ...'

'Only?' said Amanda. She was sitting opposite him now; the light behind her gleamed on her hair, ringing her with gold; her face was in shadow.

'Only sometimes now I think he resents it.'

'How could he?'

'Well, you can understand,' said Gerald. 'Feeling under a sort of obligation. Because I think he might not have made it without me. Or someone, I mean. Not me necessarily. I just happened to be there.'

'What makes you think that's how he feels?'

'Just an impression I get sometimes,' said Gerald. 'Can't explain, really. You don't know Denny.'

'No,' said Amanda. She got up and crossed to the window, and closed the curtains against the night.

'I'll tell you what he doesn't like, though,' said Gerald.

'What's that?' She remained standing at the window.

'Me coming here. He doesn't like that at all.'

'Doesn't he?' She wove the edge of the curtain between her fingers.

Gerald turned his head to look at her over the back of the settee. 'He's been a bit funny since that first time we came. I think he feels put out. You know. Excluded.'

'I expect you're imagining it.'

Gerald shook his head. 'He can see it's a special kind of thing, you and me. It is, isn't it? You feel that?'

'Yes,' said Amanda. 'Oh yes. You know I do.' Saying it smoothed the prickles of guilt that had been troubling her. She returned and sat down beside him. Denny seemed to her, at the moment, to be of very little importance.

14

It was late when Gerald got home, but Denny was still up, sitting in the kitchen just as he had left him; the dish remained on the table among its crumpled wrappings. Whatever the things were that Denny had had to do, there was no sign of his having done them.

'Hi,' he said. 'Did you have a nice time?'

'Yes,' said Gerald.

'How is she?'

'Oh, she's all right,' said Gerald, unaware that Denny had been forcing himself, for the last half-hour, to stay awake so that he could ask the question and hear it answered. Gerald did, however, find himself feeling, rather to his surprise, vaguely sorry for Denny, who had nothing in his life, so it seemed, to compare with the marvel of Amanda. 'You're right,' Gerald went on, nodding in the direction of the silver dish, 'it is a lovely thing. It sort of glows, doesn't it? – Even though it could do with a good clean,' he added.

'We are going to sell it, are we?'

'Well, of course,' said Gerald. 'Whatever it is we'll get more than you gave for it, I'd imagine. What did you think we'd do with it?'

'Oh well,' said Denny.

'Oh well what?'

'I thought we might keep it, that's all.'

'Keep it?' Gerald said, amazed. 'It's no use to us, as such, is it? Not *here*.'

'No,' said Denny. 'Did you know we had slugs?'

'You're crazy,' said Gerald. 'Of course we don't want to keep it. ... What do you mean, slugs?'

'I've been watching them,' said Denny. 'They're fascinating. They climb out from behind the draining board and eat the bits in the sink tidy. Really graceful feeders, they are.'

'That's disgusting,' said Gerald. 'I'll get something tomorrow.'

'You wouldn't mind them if they were snails,' said Denny. 'It's their nakedness puts you off.'

'I wouldn't like them whatever they were,' said Gerald. 'Pellets, that's what you get for slugs. And no leaving stuff around. Everything in the bin from now on.'

'Live and let live,' said Denny.

'Not slugs,' said Gerald. 'Let's have that, it ought to be in the safe.'

Denny had picked up the dish and was holding it clasped against his chest, protectively; but now he let it drop back on to the table as though it were of no more value to him than the scraps of newspaper around it.

'Careful,' said Gerald.

'Night,' said Denny.

Gerald went to inspect the sink. He saw no slugs, but he could clearly see the silvery tracks that they had made. 'What a dump,' he said to himself, his face crinkling with revulsion. Before he too went to bed, he emptied out the sink tidy into the bin, and collected up the scattered newspaper to cram in on top. The silver dish he locked away securely.

15

'Did he tell you about the dish?' asked Denny.

'I don't think so,' said Amanda. 'What dish?'

'He didn't, then. Well, act surprised when he does.'

'It's very exciting,' Amanda said, when Denny had finished the story. 'I hope it really is worth a lot, that would be wonderful.'

'It is, I know already,' Denny said. 'I wish now I hadn't let Gerald see it though.'

'Why ever not?'

'He's going to sell it, isn't he?'

'Well, of course,' said Amanda.

'I know. All the same.'

'What would you do with it?'

'Oh,' said Denny. 'I'd give it to you, I think, if it was mine.'

It did not occur to Amanda that he might be serious. 'Why did you say that?'

'Because I would.'

She suspected some kind of joke, possibly at her expense. 'I have a lot of things already.'

'You don't have anything like this,' said Denny. 'Wait till you see it. If you ever do, that is. Gerald'll tell you about it when he feels like it. Probably not till he finds out just what it's worth.'

Amanda, after a pause, said, 'I don't think you're fair to Gerald.'

'Very likely I'm not,' said Denny.

Amanda looked at him guardedly, wishing she knew why he had come. He was in his working clothes, stained, patched jeans with a ragged hole at one knee. She had an impulse to offer to mend them for him, which she dismissed immediately as ridiculous, but which nevertheless was with her long enough to make her colour with embarrassment, and, confusedly, she said, 'Gerald thinks ...' she paused, uncertain whether to say it after all, and then, 'he thinks you mind him coming here so much.'

Denny's face, at first curious, blanked. 'Why does he think that?'

'He feels, I don't know, I think he means that you must feel I take up too much of his time. Something like that.'

'That's what he thinks, is it?'

'Well, he didn't say that exactly, but –'

'Oh,' said Denny. 'Fancies himself, doesn't he.'

'He didn't mean it like that. I'm sure you know he didn't. Only it must make a difference.'

'Not a lot, no,' said Denny.

'You don't mind?'

'Look, Gerald can do what he likes, can't he.'

'That's all right then,' said Amanda, though she couldn't feel that it was, and persisted, 'Perhaps you think he's taking too much time off? Leaving you too much to do?'

'Oh, stop it,' he said. 'It isn't that at all.'

'It means such a lot to me, having Gerald.'

'I know, you don't have to keep on telling me.'

She was silent for a moment, then, 'There's something I think I should tell you.'

'Oh?' he said, sounding not much interested. 'What's that then?'

'Gerald was saying, the other night, you used to take drugs.'

'So what?' he said, startled and defensive.

'Nothing. I just thought you should know.'

'I'm glad you have such interesting things to talk about.' He stared, not at her, and then said abruptly, 'I'd have told you, some time, you know? Gerald didn't have to.'

'It doesn't matter,' said Amanda. 'I mean, of course it matters that you. ... But me knowing doesn't.'

'Gerald telling it does. Why did he?'

'I don't know. I can't remember. Don't be angry with him; I shouldn't have said anything I suppose. But it didn't seem fair that I should know more about you than you knew I knew.'

'I don't care what you know. But Gerald should bloody well shut up.'

'He was, more, telling me about himself, I think. It was in passing.'

'Gerald the good Samaritan,' said Denny. 'Does a lot of that, does he?'

'What?'

'Talks about himself?'

'Well, of course he does. There's so much I want to know. About his childhood, his mother. ... I want to know as much as I can. It makes him more like my brother.'

'I've heard a bit about his childhood too. I wouldn't have thought it had a lot in common with yours.'

'No, but –' she looked at him; his face was still set and distant. 'You are angry. I wish you wouldn't be.'

'I'm not angry with you.'

'Gerald –'

'I don't want to talk about Gerald, if it's all the same to you.'

'Why don't you want him to know you've been here?'

'Have you told him?'

'Of course I haven't.'

'Good. And don't let on you know about that dish, either, remember? Do you want me to go away now? I'm not being very entertaining.'

'I don't need to be entertained.'

'Shall I stay?'

'If you want to,' she said, suddenly aware that she very much did not want him to go, not just yet.

'Oh, I want to,' he said, as though that had been understood all along. There was silence for a little. 'Well, what shall we talk about?'

'Gerald says you tell fortunes. Can you? Could you tell me mine?'

'Gerald doesn't know a bloody thing about it,' Denny said with a violence that alarmed her. 'Telling fortunes is pretending to know the future and it's rubbish. I do the *I Ching*, which is self-knowledge, and that's something quite else.'

'How do you do it?'

'With coins, and there's a book. ... I'll show you sometime maybe if you really want to know.'

'It's like the Tarot?'

'The Tarot?' Denny said disparagingly, 'superstitious rubbish ... no, it's not really, I guess, but I don't go a lot on the Tarot. I don't like how Death keeps turning up. I know it doesn't always mean it, but all the same. ... Yes, I suppose the *I Ching* is a bit like.'

'And it helps you, doing it?'

'Yes. It kind of does,' he said, and she wanted to ask him how, but he had closed the shutters of his face again and she did not like to.

'Well,' she said, and he said, 'Yes. So much for that, then. Now what?'

'I don't know,' she said. 'You could always tell me about your childhood.'

'Why should I? I don't want to be your brother.' He looked at her; she could think of nothing to say. 'Anyway it's not interesting. Not like Gerald's. Very tame in comparison.'

'What were your parents like?'

'You really want to know?' He sounded incredulous. 'Very respectable. Very boring. They didn't like me much and I hated them. That's about it.'

'There must be more.'

'Not a lot, no,' he said, but went on, nevertheless, almost immediately, 'We just never liked each other really, I don't know why. Maybe people get born in the wrong family sometimes. My brother and sister were okay. No problems. I didn't like them either, naturally. My father had a garage. He sold second-hand cars. I worked in that bloody place every weekend, every holiday from the age of about twelve. For nothing, mind you. I never liked cars all that much either. It never occurred to me to ask him for anything, not for years, I must have been a bit retarded in those days, and when I finally did, he didn't say anything, just sat down and wrote out a long list of everything they'd spent on me since I'd been born, from nappies on, practically, so that was that. Then I got a bit older and I started to do terrible things like staying out after ten o'clock at night, which was not approved of, and then I went on one of the Aldermaston marches, which was the end as far as he was concerned, you couldn't sink lower. He told me he'd spent four years of his life fighting in Africa and places to make the world safe for me to grow up in, and when he looked at me and the kind of Reds and beatniks I was going round with he wished he hadn't bothered. I told him being born hadn't been my idea and anyway he'd just done what he was told and if they'd told him to shovel Jews into gas-ovens he'd have said yes sir and got on with it. He didn't like that.'

'Well, it wasn't a very nice thing to say.'

'I didn't actually mean it to be nice, you know, Amanda.'

'No,' she said.

'Anyway ... you will stop me if you get bored, won't you? Anyway, you'd have thought he'd have been pleased when I got into university, wouldn't you, I mean, no one from our family ever had. And Oxford, no one from our school, ever, I don't think. ... But that was wrong too. All he could see was three more years mucking about instead of working. I half-killed myself to get in there, I wanted to so much, to show him, but books weren't work, not the way he saw it. I expect if I'd have done something like engineering so I could've gone off afterwards and built bridges in the jungle and all that, he'd have seen the point, but as it was he said he knew more about economics running his business than I'd ever learn there, and politics was just a bunch of those Commies again talking rubbish, and it was a waste of time and taxpayers' money, and it was a pity they'd done away with National Service because that might have made something of me. It was really good to get away from home at last but it didn't work out. Getting there had been the thing, maybe. I just couldn't take it. All those really bright people, and those guys from public school. ... I kind of went to pieces so I left at the end of my second year and came to London. Are you sure I'm not talking too much?'

'You aren't,' she said. 'What did you do then?'

'Became a junky. Not straight away of course. It's not that easy. I had to work at it.'

'Don't.'

'Don't what? I'm not going into details. You can ask Gerald if you want to know. I'm sure he'll tell you.'

'I don't want to know.'

'You're probably right. It's not at all nice, really.' He began to chew at his fingernails. 'Is Gerald coming today?'

'He said he would.'

'I'll go, I think. You've probably had enough of me.'

'Are you going to give that old woman some of the money?' Amanda asked as Denny stood up.

'You what?'

'If you make a lot on the dish, will you give her some?'

'Don't let Gerald hear you say things like that. He would be shocked.'

'Seriously –'

'I am serious. I never thought of it. I know Gerald wouldn't.'

'You ought to.'

'It wasn't hers, anyway,' Denny said.

'Is that really the point? I'm sure she needs it.'

'At ninety-three she can't need much,' Denny said, off-hand.

'How can you say that?' exclaimed Amanda indignantly. 'She has to eat, she has to pay her rent and gas bills and things, can't you think what it must be like?'

'I know what it's like,' said Denny, amused, 'better than you do. She got twenty-five pounds and a clear conscience out of it, I don't reckon she's done too badly.'

'Are you sure? About the clear conscience?'

'Yes,' said Denny. 'Don't worry about it.'

An idea occurred to Amanda. 'You could go and see her sometimes. Just to make sure she's all right.'

She expected that he'd laugh at her for suggesting it, but he seemed to be considering it quite seriously. 'Would you like it if I did?' he asked. 'I must say though I'd rather come and see you.'

'You could do both.'

'Maybe I will. So long,' – and he was gone, abruptly, slamming out of the flat as if, Amanda thought, he was glad to go.

16

'You're very good to me,' said Mrs Tribe. 'There's not many that bother. You're very good.'

Denny shifted in his chair, said nothing, drank his tea; did not feel good. He would have felt much better if Mrs Tribe had shut the door in his face, as he had half-expected (hoped?) she would, the first time he had called back to see her, instead of welcoming him. 'Isn't it a good thing you went?' Amanda had said, with obvious pleasure; so he had gone again, for her sake, not for Mrs Tribe's, certainly not for his own.

Gerald was dealing with the dish. Denny didn't much want to know about it, not any more. He thought he wouldn't really care if Gerald did decide to have it melted down. Gerald hadn't told Amanda about it yet. 'Why not?' Denny asked. 'I'd rather wait,' said Gerald. 'Until we know for sure. ...'

Amanda and Gerald were looking at shops. This was something Denny was not meant to know; at least, he had not learnt about it from Gerald. 'I suppose he'll get around to mentioning it some time,' Denny said. Amanda said, reproachfully, 'If he knew I was seeing you, he'd have told me not to tell you. You can't blame him.' 'Why doesn't he want me to know, though?' said Denny. 'He doesn't have to tell you everything,' said Amanda. 'When you two open this high-class junk shop,' said Denny, and she interrupted with, 'Oh, it's nothing so definite yet.' 'Yet,' said Denny, 'are you going to employ me, I wonder?' 'I don't know why we wouldn't,' said Amanda, but there was a hesitation in her voice that made Denny think she might have some idea why not.

'Sorry?' Mrs Tribe had said something to him, and seemed to expect an answer; he'd been letting her rabbit on, without listening.

'Another cup of tea?' She pushed herself with difficulty out of her chair and shuffled to the table. Everything she did was exaggeratedly, painfully slow. Denny could hardly believe that even someone so old could find movement that hard, and was half-inclined to think that she had, over thousands of empty days, learned to spin out her actions in order to fill the time.

The pouring of two cups of tea took her the best part of five minutes, and involved a number of journeys that could have been avoided if she had at the beginning collected everything into one place. But no: she had first to empty the slops into the stone sink in one corner of the room, fetch milk (in a jug covered with a beaded cloth) from the larder, pour it, return the jug to the larder, go to the cooker where the teapot stood, carry the pot to the table in the centre of the room, pour the tea, put the pot back on the stove; all this accompanied by a muttered commentary which Denny at first found embarrassing, as though he were peering in at her without her knowledge, but which now only made him want to scream with irritation. Probably she was no longer aware that she was speaking; sometimes, in fact, she spoke without sound, her mouth moving as she carried out her unnecessary actions. On his first visit he had tried to help her but that had been a mistake, he quickly realised: she had been hurt by his implied suggestion that she could not do all this by herself. So now he only sat and watched, and sank deeper into depression.

'If it wasn't for you,' said Mrs Tribe, settled at last, 'I wouldn't have seen a soul all week. Not to talk to. They don't bother, these days. And they've no time for you in the shops. No one to tell you anything. They're all stuck behind those desks wearing out their fingers on those whatdoyoucallit, those machines, and they don't know soap from cheese except for the price stuck on.'

'That's progress,' said Denny.

'So they say,' she said. 'They tell me all this lot's going to be pulled down before long. All these houses. There's progress too I suppose.'

'This one?'

'All of them. I don't expect to be here to see it, though, not the way things go. I can't say I'm sorry. – Are you off already?'

'I've got a lot to do.'

'No peace for the wicked, they say.'

'They do say that, yes.'

Her room, he realised, smelt like the shop; he wondered how long it would be before the sagging-seated armchair and the table with the dull-red chenille cloth and the rest of the bits and pieces would be loaded into some van or other. *What is it keeps people alive*, he thought.

'Very nice of you to come, I do appreciate it, very kind. ...' It seemed to him that her gratitude pursued him down the street; if it had been tangible, he would have kicked it into the gutter to join the litter that drifted thick as fallen autumn leaves.

17

'Hey, listen to this,' said Denny, turning the radio up.

'Turn it down, can't you,' said Gerald.

'No, listen.'

'What?'

'Don't you remember it? "Singing the Blues"?' Denny hummed with it for a few bars. 'I don't know, it used to sound better. Doesn't it bring it all back though?'

'All what?'

'All that. There's something in the old nostalgia bit I guess. Don't you really remember it?' Gerald shook his head. 'I don't know. I don't know how you spent your youth. I don't think you ever did any of the normal things.'

'I don't expect I did,' said Gerald.

' "Never felt more like crying all night," ' Denny sang softly, ' "'cause everything's wrong and nothing ain't right. ..." That's it, isn't it? Says it all.'

'Does it?' said Gerald.

Denny switched the radio off. 'It's depressing though all the same.'

'What is?'

'When your youth starts turning up in collector's corner,' said Denny. 'Doesn't it make you feel old?'

'I don't feel old,' said Gerald.

'I do, sometimes, and it's just going to go on, from here. Downhill all the way. What a thought. Did you know you reached your physical peak at the age of about seventeen and a half?'

'I don't know what you're on about half the time,' said Gerald. 'The slugs seem to be eating those things I put down, but they're still around. Look, all over here.'

'I know,' said Denny. 'I watched them last night, feeding in the moonlight. A charming sight.'

'Perhaps it just takes time to work,' said Gerald.

'I wonder could you make friends with a slug.'

'What for?'

'Well, you have to have something, don't you?'

'If it goes on,' said Gerald, 'I'll ask if there's anything more effective.'

Denny, who carefully swept up the slug pellets every night after Gerald put them down, and threw them away, grinned and said nothing. The phone rang; Gerald went to answer it. Denny sat, whistling through his teeth, kicking the table leg.

'Amanda's not well,' said Gerald. 'I think I'd better get over there right away if you don't mind.'

'Oh, I don't mind,' said Denny. 'I don't mind at all.' Gerald got ready to go out. *Don't tell me, will you*, Denny thought, savagely. 'What's the matter with her, then?'

'Sounds like 'flu,' Gerald said, preoccupied. 'You can manage, can't you?'

'I'll have to, won't I?' *He looks so bloody pleased*, thought Denny, *so glad he can go rushing off to take care of her*. ... 'You aren't taking the van are you?'

'Well, I thought. ... No, I suppose you might need it.'

'I should think I almost certainly will. When will you be back?'

'I can't really say, can I?' said Gerald. 'I'll give you a ring. ... She sounded dreadful. Her temperature's way up, she's dizzy. ... I don't know when I'll be back.'

'She ought to get the doctor,' said Denny.

'She's done that,' Gerald said impatiently. 'He's coming some time this morning.'

Several times, after Gerald had left, Denny was on the point of picking up the phone to call Amanda, but in the end did not. All morning he waited for Gerald to ring, but Gerald, of course, unaware of his anxiety, was in no hurry. When he did call, mid-afternoon, it was to say that he had decided to spend the night at Amanda's. Denny was conscious, as he put the phone down, of a grinding rage inside him that would have liked to smash something to pieces.

18

Gerald sat in shadowy lamplight, hardly stirring, as though turning on more lights, or making any movement, could disturb Amanda, asleep in her room. He had done everything for her, that day: poured medicine, brought drinks, supported her on her unsteady walks to the bathroom, even – she was so limp, so disinclined to any exertion – bathed her face. 'I ought at least to be able to do this,' she said. 'But you don't have to,' he said. 'I'm here.'

It was 'flu, it was not serious, and knowing this, Gerald could be, not exactly glad that she was so fevered and weak, but at any rate grateful that he was able to be there, and that she was comforted by his presence. The attentions that he had shown her all day long were those which his mother, however much she might have needed them, would never have accepted from him. 'You make me sick,' she would have said, 'fussing me … get away.' He remembered one time when he had gone to see her (never able to stay away for long, no matter how firm his resolve, at first, to make the break, this time, final) coming into her room (the smell, the filth, how anyone could live like that) and thinking her, for a moment, dead, it was all so quiet, only the greedy buzz of blowflies on some bits of food that had been left out, until he had with relief (*had* it been relief?) heard her breathing harshly under the sheets; and he had opened the windows as wide as they could go to let some air into the sour and stifling room, and she had sat up groggily and yelled at him, and would accept nothing, only a bottle from the off-licence round the corner, which he had fetched unwillingly, but fetched all the same, because it was the only thing that she would let him do for her. … Now, and here, both so different, washed gently across his memory, began to obliterate it.

He went with careful silent steps to the door of Amanda's room, which he had left slightly ajar. She moved and sighed, as though aware of him standing there, and spoke some words in a low blurred voice; Gerald could not make them out. When he said her name she did not answer; she had spoken in her sleep. Gerald went to bed himself, in the spare room, and slept on the alert all night, in case she called him; but she slept soundly.

19

Gerald stayed three days, at the end of which he decided, reluctantly, that Amanda couldn't any longer be said to need him quite as much as she had at the beginning of her illness. She was still far from fully recovered but she assured him that she could manage now on her own. He filled the flat with everything he could think of that she could possibly want, provisions for a siege rather than for the twenty hours or so that he would be gone, and went home.

Denny was in the kitchen, sitting with his feet up on the table, eating Chinese food from a tinfoil container.

'How's everything been?' asked Gerald. 'Any problems?'

'No problems,' said Denny. 'I'd have rung, wouldn't I?'

'Good,' said Gerald.

'How is she?'

'Amanda? She's all right,' said Gerald. 'She's much better. Anything been happening?'

'Not a lot,' said Denny. 'I made a note of everything, I think.'

Gerald ran his eye down an untidy scribbled page of notes and figures. 'What's this, here?'

'That?' Denny craned his neck to see. 'That says labour. I had to get some help this morning, there was some heavy stuff I couldn't shift on my own.'

'Oh yes?' said Gerald. 'Who did you get?'

'Are you checking up on me?' Denny swung his feet on to the floor.

'Of course I'm not checking up,' said Gerald. 'I just wondered, that's all.'

Denny went on as though Gerald hadn't spoken. 'Don't you trust me?'

'Of course I trust you,' Gerald said, astonished. 'All I did was ask –'

'I've been on my own for three bloody days,' Denny said,

'working till all hours, while you've been sitting around holding Amanda's hand, and the first thing you do when you walk in here is start checking up on me.'

'Oh, forget it,' said Gerald. 'What's got into you anyway?'

Denny said nothing. He was perfectly well aware that Gerald had no misgivings about his handling the business. He had simply used the first excuse that came along to unload some of the anger that had been building up in him over the past few days.

Gerald thought, *it's unreasonable. Isn't it? It's surely obvious my place was with Amanda.* ... And then he found himself thinking, *well, if he feels like that, then maybe* ... and caught himself up, just short of ingratitude, realising that he was perhaps too eagerly latching on the reasons that would support the half-formed idea he had in his mind, that it might be as well if, some time, not immediately, but some time in the not too distant future, if for instance the still vague plans he was making with Amanda came to anything, he and Denny should part company. ... It was ungrateful to be thinking this just now, he could see, because he really didn't have any grounds for criticizing the way Denny worked. It wasn't everybody, he had to admit, who could safely be left, at a moment's notice, to get on with things ... and yet, his picture of the future had somehow no room in it for Denny.

'Look,' he said, 'I didn't mean to imply –'

'Doesn't matter,' said Denny. He shied the tinfoil container, like a frisbee, into the sink, scattering glutinous bits of rice and beansprouts on the draining board.

'That's the way to encourage the slugs,' said Gerald. 'You hadn't eaten half that.'

'Didn't want it,' said Denny. 'I think I've got an ulcer, you know.'

'You haven't got an ulcer,' said Gerald.

'How do you know what I've got or haven't got?' asked Denny. 'I get guts ache all the time.'

'You eat the wrong things,' said Gerald. 'See a doctor, why don't you, if you're worried.'

'Sympathetic, aren't you,' said Denny. 'I'm going out.'

He walked down to the tube station. There had been a market that day; the street that ran alongside the railway line was still adrift with débris, cabbage leaves and rotten oranges, cardboard boxes, plastic bags. An old man was shuffling among them, turning them over with a stick and every now and again stooping to pick up something which he placed in a carrier bag. When Denny had come this way the night before, the stalls had been standing ready, empty and skeletal. He had spent part of the evening, for no good reason, outside the building where Amanda lived. He had no hope of seeing her, though for a time he deluded himself with the thought that Gerald might, just possibly, leave. ... For an hour or so he had watched the lighted windows of the flat, until his romanticism had sickened him. On the way home, among the vacant market stalls, he had been approached by a teenage, even, he suspected, as though it mattered, school-age whore, and was enough disgusted with his loony vigil to attempt to dull the memory of it by a brief coupling in a nearby garage, on a mattress in the back of a van. The girl had a wodge of bubble-gum in her mouth which from time to time she chewed on, absent-mindedly; he had found this a little disconcerting, but less so than her occasional perfunctory wriggling. ... It had done him no good at all; afterwards he thought, *it proves I still can, that's all, as if that was worth proving* ... and then *my sister's kids are older than that now.* ...

Tonight though Gerald was safely back at home; there was a point to his visit. He rang the bell, and rang it again, after a little while, when there was no answer, suddenly alarmed by the thought that she was no longer there: spirited away, fairy-tale-fashion, by Gerald. No: she had been sleeping. She let him in, sounding muzzy and bewildered.

'Go back to bed, Amanda.'

'No, I'm all right.'

She had a pale, drained look, like something underwater. He thought, *how can she look so terrible and still be all I ever want to see?* His heart twisted; he said, 'I only came to find out how you were.'

'Oh,' she said, without the energy, even, to wonder why he

had not already learnt this from Gerald. 'I really am much better now. It was just the first day or so that was bad, I felt like death. ...' She smiled, remembering how, not all that long ago, she would have welcomed the feeling; but Denny, for the first time in his life experiencing, at the linking of another's name with death, the vision of the abyss that attends the thought of one's own, shuddered to see her smile and hear her talk of it so lightly.

20

The dish had been sold, and Gerald was over the moon about it. It had made more than he had ever dared to hope: that was marvellous in itself, of course, at any time he would have been thrilled by such good fortune, there'd never been anything like it; but there was a particular excitement attending it now, because it made any venture he might go into with Amanda just that much less one-sided. He felt much as he had on the day he had first met her: restless, exalted, full of boundless possibilities. And Denny, just as he had been then, seemed now singularly unmoved, even, Gerald thought, morose.

'Of course,' he said, in case Denny hadn't understood him, 'half's yours. You found the thing.'

Denny shrugged his shoulders, without noticeable enthusiasm. 'I'm not bothered.'

Gerald stared: there was no making him out sometimes. Especially since he'd been so possessive about the dish to start with. 'You have to be joking,' he said. 'Anyway, it's yours.'

Now that Amanda was quite well again, Gerald asked her to come over. He had still not told her about the dish; he planned a surprise. At first it seemed to him it didn't matter, any more, about the general air of seediness that hung like dust everywhere; but as the hour of her arrival drew nearer, he began to worry that she would be disappointed, worse still, that she would think he had built things up too much: although he'd tried to be honest, he had to admit that sometimes, perhaps, when he talked to her, his ambitions had coloured reality. When he looked around him his spirits sank. Junk, most of it, old rubbish, like Denny said. Almost he wished that she was not coming, that he could have gone on keeping her apart from this, until the time, if it should ever come, when he himself could cut free. … He need not have worried, though. She came like a traveller to foreign lands (as indeed she was, for what could ever have brought her to this part of London before?) prepared to wonder at everything she saw: she could not be disappointed.

'Your car'd be better in the yard,' said Gerald, springing out to meet her as she arrived. 'Round here, anything that isn't nailed down, … I'll do it if you like. You go on in.'

Amanda found Denny in the kitchen. He was sorting through the contents of a cardboard box and barely glanced at her as she came in; she was not to know that he dared not, for fear that she might read too clearly in his face the disturbance that the sight of her, here, caused in him. She was grateful for the chance that let them meet alone; the thought that they must do so as conspirators in front of Gerald had not been pleasant. So that they might already be talking when Gerald did arrive, she said hastily, 'What's that?'

'Nothing much,' Denny said, and started to sweep the cluttered objects on the table back into their box. 'Just some old guy's bits of things. Not much here at all really.'

'Is that a medal?'

'Yes. D.S.M. It isn't anything, they all got it. All the same, you think the family might have kept it, wouldn't you? They're not things to buy and sell, are they?'

Amanda looked quickly over her shoulder; Gerald was not here yet. 'I wouldn't have imagined you'd think like that.'

'Oh.' He shifted the medal awkwardly from hand to hand before dropping it in the box. 'Well, I wouldn't keep my father's medals, that's for sure, but if I was going to be around when he was buried I'd like to see them buried with him. It's personal, that sort of thing, isn't it? It all is, come to that, all this stuff. I don't see anyone else has got a right to it at all.'

'But you buy and sell things like that all the time,' said Amanda.

'I know,' said Denny. 'Maybe I'm in the wrong job.'

'Haven't you got that lot put away yet?' said Gerald, coming in. 'What's that about being in the wrong job?'

'If I had my way,' said Denny, more in continuation of his conversation with Amanda than in answer to Gerald's question, 'there wouldn't be any of this. None of it. The Pharaohs had the right idea. Your possessions buried with you. That's what ought to happen.'

'Slaves and wives, too, didn't they?' said Gerald.

'Well, that's not necessary. That's taking it too far. But things, oh yes, definitely. Everything.'

'So wasteful, though,' said Amanda. 'And what a loss. All that beauty, underground. ...'

'And a curse on all grave-robbers,' said Denny. 'Which is what we are, I suppose.'

'I don't think you believe half the things you say,' said Gerald.

'Think of what we'd miss,' Amanda said, 'all the treasures. ... You wouldn't have had that silver dish if –' she stopped so suddenly that there was no possibility of Gerald's not catching her meaning. She looked quickly and helplessly at Denny. To her surprise he was grinning.

'You forgot you didn't know about that, didn't you,' he said.

'You told her?' said Gerald.

'Well, I didn't know you hadn't.'

'Yes, but –'

'– So when she came in I naturally said, well, what do you think about it, then, and that's how it got out.'

'I wanted to surprise you,' Gerald said, regretfully.

'Sorry,' said Denny; finding, against expectation, that he really was. There was no need to tarnish Gerald's pleasure. Things were quite interesting enough without that. 'I said she'd better not let on she knew.'

'No,' said Gerald. 'It's just as well really. I wouldn't want you to pretend.'

'Anyway, I think it's marvellous,' Amanda said.

'You ought to have seen it though,' said Denny. 'It was lovely.'

'It doesn't matter,' she said. Something in Denny's voice made her suspect that he was enjoying Gerald's ignorance, and she felt uneasy. She was glad when he said no more.

Gerald had been cast down by the misfiring of his surprise and scarcely had the heart now for the tour of the premises that he had planned; but Amanda insisted on it, and showed such interest, admiring everything that could be admired, asking questions, that he soon recovered his good humour. He fetched out for her all the things he had put by, the better things he wasn't parting with just yet, because some time, maybe ... After a little while, he opened the bottle of sherry that he had bought, most unusually, because this was after all an occasion. 'To the future,' he said, sipping it, and watching Amanda, who smiled at him as though she saw, crystal-clear, all that was in his mind's eye.

'I was thinking,' he continued, 'this morning, I thought, wouldn't it be good to have a holiday?'

'What's that?' said Denny.

Gerald ignored him; to Amanda he said, 'I mean, go abroad some place, what do you think? Somewhere warm, it would do you good.'

'I see,' she said, 'you mean –'

'The Algarve, maybe, that's meant to be very nice. We could all go, why not?' Just at the moment he felt it wouldn't be so bad, really, if Denny came along. They all deserved to celebrate, it would be friendly. 'What about it?' he said to Denny.

'No thanks,' Denny answered shortly.

'Why not?' Gerald insisted. He thought Denny might have sounded pleased to be asked, anyway, whether he wanted to come or not.

'Don't want to,' Denny said.

'It would be a break.'

'I think it would be a bloody bore.'

'You don't have to be like that,' said Gerald, offended.

Amanda said quickly, 'It was the hardest thing in the world

to get my father to take a holiday. He was never really happy with nothing to do.'

Gerald laughed. 'That isn't Denny's problem.'

'Well, thanks a lot,' said Denny.

'I didn't mean –'

'Sometimes,' Amanda said, 'I used to manage to persuade him to take a few days off and we'd go to our cottage in Wales, but once he'd finished all the work there was to do on it, he couldn't enjoy himself there. He couldn't relax. He'd walk for hours, wearing himself out, and be unhappy because there was no point to it.'

'I *didn't* mean that,' Gerald was saying to Denny, 'and you know it.'

'It sounded like it,' said Denny. 'Anyway, I don't personally think it's such a big deal, work, I mean.'

'He enjoyed it,' said Amanda. 'That was just how he was.'

'Well, I could do with a break,' said Gerald. 'Denny can please himself. What do you think about it?'

'I think it's a lovely idea,' said Amanda.

Oh, lovely, thought Denny, *really terrific.* He couldn't decide whether it would be worse to be with Gerald and Amanda, or to be alone and think about them being together. ... He listened to them discussing possibilities, and raged inwardly.

The whole of Southern Europe was reviewed, and the North African coast; conversation flagged. 'I'm so glad,' Amanda said, into the silence that hung in the air like dust, 'that I'm here at last. It has been strange, somehow, all this time, knowing you and not knowing the place where you live.'

'Well,' said Gerald, 'you can see why I wasn't exactly anxious for you to come here. I mean, it's not –'

'Has Gerald told you about the slugs?' asked Denny.

'Denny,' Gerald said, warningly.

'Slugs?' said Amanda.

'In here,' said Denny, 'at night. Our little pets. Gerald puts down pellets for them and they gobble them up and come back wagging their tails for more. They must be a new breed that thrives on poison.'

'Do you have to?' Gerald said, mortified.

'Superslug,' said Denny.

Amanda laughed, from nervousness rather than from real amusement. Denny's presence, and his mood, were troubling. She wished he had not been there.

'Shakespeare was lyrical about snails,' said Denny, 'but he never mentioned slugs, not once. It doesn't seem fair.'

'I wish you'd stop talking about slugs,' said Gerald. He wanted to be angry but he had seen Amanda laugh and thought she would not like him to be.

'Okay,' said Denny. He decided that he had had enough of being with Amanda and Gerald. He went out, and spent the whole evening wishing he had stayed.

'You see what I mean,' said Gerald. 'He's like that all the time. I think. ...'

'What?' said Amanda.

'I don't know. Maybe he'd do better, somewhere else. Don't you think?'

'I couldn't possibly say.'

'I know you couldn't. Still. ...'

'It's because of me?'

'It could be. Could be anything. Don't worry about it –'. she looked for a moment so distressed that he hastened to reassure her, 'It's just him, he's like that. It really doesn't matter. ...'

21

'Well, I'm sorry,' said Denny; not sounding it.

'Gerald was trying to be nice, you know.'

'I know.'

'Wouldn't you like to come, if we do go? It would be a way of, oh, of stopping all this; it's ridiculous, it can't go on ...' Amanda had made up her mind that she was not going to have a repeat of yesterday, ever again. She had felt like a shuttlecock, batted back and forth between the two of them, never knowing one minute where she would be the next, or if a mistimed shot might not knock her to the ground. Until then, she had not found it hard to persuade herself that seeing Denny could have no effect on her relationship with Gerald. For her, Gerald and Denny had existed in separate worlds, never touching. Yesterday had shown her how mistaken she had been in this. She had the feeling that there were things happening out of sight which she could not understand but which were nevertheless somehow her fault. It was an impossible and unnecessary situation; she could not think why she had let it start, much less continue.

'I don't want to; I already told you,' said Denny.

'But why not?'

'Well,' Denny said, 'if you really want to know, I think, if we were all together, for all that time, I think it would start being obvious what I feel for you.' He hadn't planned to say it. He had not at any time pictured himself actually telling her. *It can't go on.* … Perhaps those words had drawn it out of him. Whatever had caused him to say it, the fact that he had done so frightened him. He looked at her; she stared back, blankly, and said nothing. He thought, *she has to say something*; but she remained silent, for so long that at last he said, almost impatiently, 'Of course you've realised by now that I love you.'

She shook her head. What he had said sounded so strange to her that she was not able to feel surprise, only bewilderment.

'I don't know why you think I've been coming here all this time, then.'

I don't know either, you just came, that's all, there didn't seem to be any need to wonder why … 'I thought you were just being kind. Something like that. …'

'Oh yes,' he said. 'Sure. Mrs Tribe one day, you the next . … You can't really be that stupid, can you?'

It looks as though I can . … But when you're here it never seems as if you really want to be. … 'I'm sorry.'

'I'm so kind,' he said, 'so nice, when you were ill, you know what I wanted? I wanted you to have no one at all, not Gerald, no one, if I couldn't be there.'

'I didn't know.' *One ought to know something like that.* …

'No, of course you didn't,' he said. 'Well … there's not a lot of point me staying, is there, after that?' Amanda did not speak. She was wondering if there was any point to anything; the whole world seemed suddenly meaningless. 'I might as well go, then,' Denny went on, standing up, making each movement last as long as possible, as though he hoped, somehow, to draw some reaction from her. 'You don't have to worry, I won't be back, I don't expect I'll even. ... It does make things a lot simpler, I suppose, for everyone.'

But it doesn't at all, she thought, watching him. She still found it difficult to comprehend what he had told her, and she repeated the words to herself, trying to discover what they meant to her. Over and over again she had the sensation of travelling too fast in a lift: parts of her were left behind. She saw that Denny had reached the door – time had stretched itself out, dream-style, but he was, at last, there, would, in a moment, be gone, and it was easy to understand that much of what he had said, that he would not be coming back, ever, and the thought appalled her, twisted a knot of fear tightly in her stomach, but she could not say or do anything to prevent him going.

'Of course,' he said, turning, with his hand on the door, 'you don't feel anything like that about me.' A statement, not a question.

'Yes,' she said, so softly that he might almost not have heard her; she wondered if she hoped that he might not.

He stared at her with an expression of amazement that Amanda, if she had been at all inclined to do so, could have found comic, but did not; indeed, she scarcely saw it: there was such confusion in her senses that she could no longer be sure of what she saw or heard or felt. 'What do you mean?' he asked.

She could barely remember now what she had said, much less what she had meant. 'Yes,' she said again, 'I mean, yes, I do. ...' He did not move, and she said, 'You aren't going, are you?'

'Of course I'm not,' he answered in a slow dazed dreamer's voice, 'no, not if you. ...' He crossed the room and sat beside her, and cautiously, as though there were something between them that he might disturb or damage by too abrupt a movement, put his arm around her.

Is this what I meant? she thought. *It must be.* ... She leaned against him suddenly and so completely that for a moment he was afraid that she had fainted; but when he moved his head to look at her he saw that her eyes were open. He began to kiss her forehead, her cheek, her mouth. Her hands rested on his shoulders, without pressure, neither clasping nor repelling. Like someone who decides that it is after all better to be carried by the tide instead of struggling against it, she had for the moment stopped trying to find precise definitions for what was happening to her, within her. There was one thing at least, though, that seemed to her more clear now than ever, and after a little she said (finding it strange that she could talk still, indeed do anything that she had been used to do, before), 'We have to tell Gerald.'

'Gerald?' The tone of his voice suggested that this was the last thing he wanted to think about at present.

'We can't *not* tell him, now.' She sat upright, pulling away from him.

'I suppose we've got to,' he said, grudgingly, and then – it sounded as though he had only at that moment become aware of the reality of the last few minutes – 'I don't know what I can say to him about this.'

'It isn't fair on him if we –'

'All right,' he said, 'all *right*, I know …' and reached for her again. She grew tense in his grasp and remained so until he said, softly and plausibly, 'Of course we've got to, we'll have to think of the best way of putting it … only not now, Amanda, please, not now …'

22

Not then; not in the days and weeks that followed. Telling Gerald was an impossibility: Amanda's mind could not begin to put together the necessary words. In any case, it never seemed to be the right time to do so, when she was with him: how can you suddenly, from nothing, produce something like that? And almost, then, there seemed to be no need for it. Gerald's presence pushed Denny to the periphery of her existence. The things she talked about and did with Gerald had a solid reassuring reality. He carried her along on the wave of his enthusiasm as they made plans, visited estate agents and inspected premises to let. She took out books from the library and read about clothes, toys, bygones, ephemera. Sometimes with Gerald, but just as often on her own, she went to sales, museums, markets; she looked, listened, found out more each day. She could not remember a time in her life when she had had so much to interest her. Occasionally she thought about her father and was amazed to find how little was left of all her loss and sorrow. The past was over and done with, gathering dust. The future that glistened before her was the future seen through Gerald's eyes: she could imagine no other.

And yet Denny was there; she could not ever totally lose sight of him, although it was strange, she thought sometimes, that he seemed almost less real now than he had been before: as though love had cut through the string that bound their relationship to the actual world, leaving it adrift in fantasy. Each time they met was the same as every other. It was like a recurrent dream, real enough, while she was dreaming it, for her to leave questions unasked. It had no connection with her waking life; when it was gone, it was as if it had never been, except that she woke from it depressed and a little guilty, though by what and of what she could not quite tell. Sometimes she found herself thinking of Denny in a detached, one might almost say impersonal way, and it would seem to her then that she could, after all, very well live without him; and yet she remembered feeling, even though she could not always feel, how unbearable the thought of losing him had been, without knowing, precisely, what it was that she would have lost; and every time she saw him she was caught again in the meshes of a melancholy and aimless longing.

Love, he had said. *I love you*; she had seemed to hear the words not with her ears but with her whole body: she might have been made of glass and his voice pitched precisely to set her ringing. *It must be*, she thought, *what I feel, it must be* ... but she could not be sure, because she did not know how love, that sort of love, ought to feel. Her emotions had become alien to her: curiously misplaced. It was as if she only missed Denny when he was with her. She could not believe that this was how it was supposed to be.

Their time together was spent largely in silence. Amanda could not often think of what to say and besides it did not seem to her that Denny wanted to talk. He held and kissed her or lay with his head in her lap and was content with silence; she would touch his face and hair, and try to make sense of her confused feelings. She found it odd that touching did not bring them closer to each other: she had thought that it must do.

As for Denny: though he had apparently agreed with Amanda that Gerald had to be told, now more than ever, he didn't in fact at all want or intend to do it. He found it delightful to return from seeing Amanda and know that Gerald had no inkling where he had been or what he had been doing. He liked to imagine the effect that knowing would have on Gerald, and wasn't in any hurry to spoil his own pleasure by handing Gerald that knowledge.

Gerald could study travel brochures all he liked, or keep in his desk, not shown to Denny, but discovered by him all the same, a folder with details from estate agents, scribbled with notes; it didn't matter much, since Denny could always use for comfort the thought of Amanda, her mouth, her hands on his, and better still, her willingness to conspire with him in keeping Gerald unaware.

His days did not seem complete if they did not give him time, however short, spent with her; because of Gerald, he had many incomplete days. He counted hours, raced headlong across London whenever the chance offered itself of a few moments with her, and fretted when it did not. Each time he saw her he was immediately conscious of how soon he would have to leave her, and however much he wanted, needed, to see and touch her, he found no real and lasting satisfaction in their meetings. He felt as though he was getting nowhere, without in the least knowing where it was that he wanted to go.

It was twenty years since he had felt anything like this;

although no, this was not the same as the way he had felt in adolescence, when lust and adoration had been separate but not for all that incongruous; when exaggerated and romantic worship of the ground a girl walked on, the air she breathed, had not prevented another part of his mind plotting how to get his hands inside her knickers (hers, or anyone's, who'd help him satisfy his desire and curiosity, it wasn't all that important). He had no curiosity left now; he had swum through what had once seemed darkly splendid and mysterious waters but which now appeared to him, from the sandbank on which he lay beached, to be muddy and brackish and not worth the crossing. And as for desire ... Amanda was constantly in his mind, but his vision of her was not a sensual one. His kisses were undemanding; even in his thoughts he asked nothing more from her. But, in the last few weeks, his dreams had become increasingly erotic. They were not of her. He could not remember, on waking, that they had been about anyone. Dreams of unfocused desire, which sometimes spent itself while he was still asleep, and sometimes stung him into half-conscious wakefulness, to satisfy it mechanically, with an empty mind; this over, his thoughts could once again open themselves to her.

It was only Gerald who was not troubled by dreams of any kind. Nothing rose from the depths of his mind to ripple or to cloud the surface. For the first time in his life he had what he wanted. He knew that what Amanda had said about her father – their father – was true also of him. Nothing he had done up till now had had any point or value because it had been done for no one (for his mother, yes, at first, he'd tried, he'd wanted to prove to her what he could do and be, but that had been as useful as beating his head against the wall). Now, with Amanda beside him, he felt confident of success in anything he chose to do. Just as soon as he was clear of this place (he glared around him as though he could, by mental power alone, bring the whole building crashing down in ruins). He heard Denny upstairs, playing records, and he thought, *he's no problem. When the time comes we can deal with him.*

23

'What do you think about this one, then?' asked Gerald.

Amanda began to read the sheet of paper that he handed her, and though her eyes and part of her brain took in the words, she was at the same time wondering, as she had been before he spoke, *it is strange, though, isn't it, that he hasn't noticed anything? As if nothing at all had changed. I thought that love was supposed to transform people, somehow. So that nobody could help noticing. Yet we still go on just the same.* ... 'Yes,' she said, 'yes, it sounds like the sort of place we're looking for.'

'There's a flat above it,' Gerald said.

'Yes,' she said, 'I saw.' *Perhaps that's just in stories, though. I wouldn't know. Poetry. ... I can't really see how I could be different. Or him. What would.* ... She realised, from Gerald's expression, that he was expecting her to say more. 'I'm sorry, I was just ...,' she said, and made a pretence of studying the paper again.

'Do you think we should go and have a look at it?'

'Oh, definitely,' she said, and felt it comforting to be definite about something. Thinking about Denny was like trying to fish fragments of shell from a bowlful of broken eggs; he slid from her cautiously groping mind each time she thought that she had secured him. How could she imagine him changed when she could not properly imagine him at all, before, since, at any time? 'Don't you?' she asked Gerald.

'I was just wondering what you thought about the flat.'

'The flat? Oh. ...' She let Denny slide back uncaught although the knowledge that he was still there continued to trouble her, vaguely. 'Well ... you'll need somewhere, won't you?'

'I was thinking about you.'

'Me?'

'If you'd ever considered moving. ...'

'Oh. ...' The possibility of choosing where she lived had

never occurred to her; she was amazed, now, that it had not, and she looked briefly around at what had suddenly become to her a prison, now that she realised that she was free to make that choice.

'Or if. …' Gerald, clearly, was balancing on the edge of an idea, deterred, perhaps, from plunging by Amanda's air of not being altogether in the same place as himself.

'What?' She looked directly at him; he toppled.

'If you liked being on your own. If you wouldn't rather. … We could find somewhere big enough. This one might. …'

'To share, you mean?'

'Yes,' he said. 'Well … it's a thought, isn't it?'

'Would you like that?'

'Yes.'

'Then let's,' she said. It seemed so obvious, now that he said it, that she found no need to consider it, although she could not remember ever having thought of it before. 'I really don't like living here,' she went on. 'I've never liked it all that much. And now it seems so big and empty. I'd so much rather not be alone.'

'If you're sure about it then,' he said, 'well, that's what we'll look out for.'

But what about Denny? Amanda wondered, surprised that it had taken so long for him to reappear on the surface of her mind. *That would have to make a difference, wouldn't it?* 'What about Denny?' she said, this time aloud, to Gerald, in case he too had forgotten him, 'I mean –'

'Denny?' said Gerald. 'Oh, he isn't any problem.'

'Isn't he?'

'Of course not. He'll manage.'

'Have you told him about this? What does he think?'

'Naturally I haven't. Not before talking to you.'

'You'll tell him now?'

'There's no hurry.'

'But. …'

'What?'

'He's your friend,' said Amanda. *And haven't you really noticed any change in him? It seems so.* … 'Oughtn't you to –'

'I don't think he is, really,' said Gerald, thoughtfully, 'no, I wouldn't call him that. I don't think it's up to him to think anything of it one way or another. It's not as if. ... We haven't all that much in common, you know. There's a lot about me he doesn't understand. Couldn't possibly.'

'Well, if you don't *talk* to him –'

'There's no point. Like about you and me. He doesn't really get that at all. He thinks ... well, he still thinks it's the money I'm interested in; he's said as much.'

'He can't really –'

'Oh yes. And let's face it. A lot of people would. It worried me at one time that you might.'

'Think that? Oh no.' *That's right, I suppose people would. How ridiculous. It never entered my mind. ... But Denny doesn't think that at all, I'm sure. ...* 'Does it still worry you?'

'Not any more. Not knowing you. ... You see – explaining's hard, isn't it? What one feels. Impossible. But with you I don't have to. You understand.'

You, she thought, *yes, I think so. But myself, that's another matter entirely. It would be a lot simpler if it was just you and me. ...*

'You see,' said Gerald, 'if I use the word love,' Amanda felt her thoughts quiver and scatter like beads of mercury, 'well, I can, to you; you know what I mean by it. But other people. They've no idea. Denny, for instance. *He* doesn't know what it is.'

'I'm not so sure that I do,' said Amanda, and wished immediately that she had not. Gerald's belief in her fed her own sense of identity; she was afraid to damage it.

It was, however, strong enough. 'Oh, you do,' he said with conviction. 'If it has to be put into words, it's caring for another person more than for yourself. Isn't it? I mean, we both know what that's like. Wanting to give. ... Only, when the person you love doesn't want to know, like my mother, well ...'

'Yes,' she said. 'Yes, I can understand what that's like too, a little. ... I was never as important to my father as he was to me.'

Gerald nodded. 'It hurts, doesn't it?'

'I don't mean that I went through anything like you did; because he did care about me, I always knew that. I kept telling myself that.'

'Ought you to have to keep telling yourself, though?' asked Gerald.

'No, I suppose not. I wanted, you see, not to be like my mother was. Always asking for more. More of his time, more … I don't know. Affection, perhaps? He wasn't very demonstrative … I thought she wanted too much from him. I thought maybe if she hadn't asked so much he might have given more. I used to think we would be happier without her, sometimes. I'd imagine our life if she wasn't there. No arguments … I disliked her so much sometimes for spoiling things. She seemd to take everything the wrong way. Complained so much. … And yet when she was ill she said nothing about it, nothing at all. We didn't know. At least I didn't. And then she went into hospital, quite suddenly, and it was all over very quickly. … I couldn't exactly feel sorry, though I thought I should, but I do remember feeling that it was somehow my fault.'

'It couldn't have been.'

'No, but you do feel that, don't you? In any case, it was more that I had the feeling she wanted me to think it was my fault. … That must sound so silly.'

'No,' Gerald said.

'Anyway, afterwards, I tried very hard to be, well, as I thought she should have been. I still felt she'd been wrong, not to be satisfied with what she had. Her death didn't change that. And I went on not liking her even after she wasn't there, because he … well, he never really got over it. He didn't talk about her, but … I'd think, how can he miss her, the way she used to go on at him, he must see that everything's better now. I suppose I didn't understand there was more between them than I could see. … I think love's a very complex thing really.'

'It doesn't have to be,' said Gerald. 'Of course, when people are married, there's obviously. … But, I mean, my mother, she thought love was something, well, something you do, you know? It really isn't. It's so unnecessary, most of it. Like animals, but worse, because animals don't think about it. And people think they have to, that it matters somehow. It doesn't. They don't have to.'

Even before she gathered Gerald's meaning, Amanda found herself infected by his embarrassment, and was thrown into further confusion by the thought of Denny entering her mind suddenly and uninvited. She could not think of anything to say.

'I know,' said Gerald, 'I don't much like talking about it. It seems to be everywhere, these days. Pushed at you. As if it was the only thing.'

'Don't you think though,' said Amanda, 'that it can be part of love?'

'It isn't what *I* mean by love,' said Gerald. 'I know what some people would say about what I felt about my mother. Freud. All that. It's rubbish.'

'All the same. ...' said Amanda, and was not sure how to continue, 'It confuses things so much, though, because –'

'That's just it,' said Gerald, without waiting to hear her out. 'Confuses. I knew you understood. It all ought to be so simple. Can be. If you forget about all that. Listen. Denny thinks I'm abnormal because I've never. ... Well. I don't know about normal. But some of the things he's told me. ... It's revolting. As though people were machines.'

'What do you mean?' Amanda asked after a pause. 'What things?'

'I'd rather not,' said Gerald. 'And you don't really want to hear. You know anyway. You just have to read the papers, turn on the television. No one can be ignorant, these days.'

'You mean he tells you things like that about himself?'

'Used to. Not any more,' said Gerald. 'No. He can do what he likes, I suppose, but I can't listen to all that. – I don't know why we're talking about it.'

'We were talking about love,' said Amanda.

'Love,' said Gerald. 'For some people that's all it is. I mean, Denny, if you used the word that's what he'd think of. Nothing else.'

'But –' Amanda began, and stopped, shifting her thoughts from speech to silence, *that isn't what he thinks of, not at all, not with me. He hardly touches me. I think I wish he would.* ... For how long she could not be sure the idea had hung like a cloud in the corner of her mind, growing and darkening without her much being aware of it; but now it was as though the first drops of rain falling had at last alerted her to its presence.

Gerald was still speaking. 'I don't care how much he's *done*, he doesn't *know* a thing, not about love.'

What does he want from me then? thought Amanda. *And what does he mean when he says love?*

'I'll tell you something though,' said Gerald. 'I try to understand him. I make the effort. I've listened. But talking to him: like a blank wall. I couldn't get through, not in a million years. That's him, not me. I can get you to understand what I mean. It's minds, you see, that are important. Where they touch. That's what matters.'

'What have we got bodies for, then?' asked Amanda. She spoke lightly, making a joke of it, because she very much wanted the conversation to be over; but at the same time she thought she would like to know the answer to the question, if there was one. 'Are they just things we use for carrying our minds around in?'

'Something like that,' said Gerald, considering the words. 'Yes, that's a good way to put it. I think that's exactly what they are.'

24

Amanda's solicitor looked at her across the desk; dropped his eyes to glance briefly at the papers in front of him. There were faint lines of concern creasing his forehead.

'Who are they?' Amanda said, repeating his question. 'Friends.'

'Yes, but. ...'

'You said I ought to make a will. I can't think of anyone else.'

'I hope you don't mind me asking,' he said, 'but I feel –'

'I don't mind,' said Amanda. 'I don't see there's any problem, though.'

'Oh, no problem' he said. 'Mm ... have you known them long?'

'For some time,' said Amanda.

'I see,' he said. 'Yes, well. ...'

'Gerald and I are in fact thinking of going into business together,' she said. It sounded suddenly so unlikely, hearing herself telling someone else about it, in this assured and formal atmosphere; she half-expected him to say, *really, my dear, you can't possibly do anything like that* ... and to forestall him, added, 'I shall probably be asking advice on various matters, once our plans are a little more definite'. (*Was that the right thing to say? Do I sound like someone who knows what she's doing?*)

'Are you really, Amanda?' (*Is he surprised? Was there an indulgent note in his voice?*) 'What sort of thing did you have in mind?'

'We're thinking of running an antique shop.'

'I had no idea you knew about such things.'

'I'm learning,' she said.

'It's a chancy business, you know. Without experience –'

'Gerald has the experience.'

'And you're going to finance it, is that the idea?' he asked sharply.

'We both are,' she said. The defensiveness that put an edge to her voice could have been mistaken for decisiveness. 'I can't do nothing for the rest of my life, after all, can I? Since I do have money, I might just as well use it to do something that interests me.'

'I wouldn't try to dissuade you from doing *that*,' he said. 'Only, I can't help feeling, perhaps ... advice –'

'I told you I'd ask for it,' she said, 'when I want it.'

He laughed. 'You sound very like your father.'

'He was usually right about things. Even when other people thought he wasn't.'

'And you think that you take after him?'

'I don't know,' she said. 'I'll never know unless I try, shall I?'

'We shall see,' he said. 'Well ... we'll get this drawn up. And later, when', he smiled, 'you want advice, I'll be most happy to do all I can.'

'Thank you,' she said.

'Perhaps,' he paused as though weighing something up in his mind, 'we might have lunch together sometime. You could tell me what you've been learning about antiques. A fascinating subject, I believe.'

'I'd like that very much,' she said.

The smile with which she said goodbye to him lingered on her face as she left the office. She was delighted with herself. For the first time in her life she felt on equal terms with someone from her father's world, and the thought exhilarated her: she walked briskly, wishing she could run. It seemed to her that she had become, somehow, noticeable, that the people she passed must be turning to look at her. She felt extraordinarily self-conscious, in a totally pleasing way. After a little, it occurred to her that some at least of this feeling might be due to her having grown aware, during the last few moments of their meeting, that her solicitor really rather admired her. Something about his look, a certain warmth in his voice, a final handshake firmer and more prolonged than strictly necessary: she thought how strange it was that these should give her a greater realisation of her attractiveness than Denny ever did. As always, the recollection of Denny sent her mind spinning into confusion, and her smile faded gradually like the withdrawing of light from the sky at evening.

25

Amanda had read in the paper about two old women, sisters, recluses for half a century, who had died recently within a week of each other. It occurred to her that there might be things in their house that would be worth trying to get hold of.

'You're wasting your time,' Denny said when she rang. 'The vultures will have already descended.'

'Is Gerald there?' she asked. 'I'd like to know what he thinks.'

Gerald thought, really, much as Denny did, but he did not

want to dampen Amanda's enthusiasm. 'We could try, anyway,' he said. 'Better be right now, if we're going to, hadn't it.'

'You can't take the van,' Denny said sulkily. 'I need it today.'

'We're going in her car,' Gerald said. 'I know. There won't be anything to bring back, but she wants to go, so. ...'

Gerald and Amanda drove out of London to the town where the old women had lived. He was amazed at Amanda's persistence and her powers of persuasion as they tracked down, through neighbours, undertakers, solicitors, the nephew who now owned the house and its contents. As Gerald had expected, most of the things had already been carted away. He had guessed as much when they had first seen the house with its curtainless windows and a half-filled skip standing outside.

'Isn't there anything left?' asked Amanda. 'Anything at all?'

'Bits of rubbish,' said the nephew. 'Broken stuff. Clothes.'

'Clothes?' said Amanda, not over-eagerly.

'All old things, mind,' said the nephew. 'I don't think they'd bought anything in fifty years. They never left the house, you know. They were a bit, well. ...' he tapped his forehead.

'I like old clothes,' Amanda said. 'Could we have a look?'

'That's if they're still there,' said the nephew. 'I've had the builders in, you know, getting some idea if it's worth renovating. I rather think they're going to suggest the whole lot comes down. It's a good site. Get half a dozen nice little maisonettes there.'

There were holes in the walls where laths showed through like bones, broken floorboards left gaping holes, the banisters sagged. Thick dust, grimy grey and plaster white, hung everywhere, choking the air. There was a damp and sweetish smell. 'Dry rot,' the nephew said, kicking a collapsing banister. 'Rising damp. You name it. They did nothing to the place.'

'Did you see much of them?' asked Amanda.

'Never saw them in my life that I can remember. They were, what's the word, hermits. And cracked, like I said. The one that died first, you know, the other one just left her in her bed. Didn't tell anyone. And then next week the groceries never got taken in, so someone came round to have a look.' He laughed.

'Course I was hoping they'd have stacks of sovereigns tucked under the bed but no such luck.'

'Was there much?' asked Gerald. 'I mean, furniture, ornaments, that sort of thing?'

'Oh. Nothing special. Nothing I'd want in the house. That's all gone, anyway.'

'I don't suppose,' said Gerald, 'things like postcards, theatre programmes ...?'

'You a dealer?'

'We like old things,' Amanda said.

'Yes? Well, anything like that's gone. Left the clothes because my wife said Oxfam. I said, you're joking, and when she had a look she agreed with me. They could be here still.'

They were; cardboard boxes piled up in one of the bedrooms, badly packed and bulging. 'Can we have a look?' asked Amanda.

'You can take the lot,' he said. 'And I do mean the lot. It'll save me a trip to the rag merchant.'

'How much do you want for it?' Gerald asked.

'We ought to have a look at it first though,' said Amanda.

'Look, I don't want to hang about,' the nephew said. 'What's it worth to you?'

'What do you think, Gerald?'

'I don't know,' said Gerald. 'Risk ten pounds, if you're really keen, I suppose, Amanda. Okay? That's more than they'd fetch as rags.'

'Kind of hobby, is it?' the man asked.

'That's right,' Amanda said. 'Are you sure we want to spend ten pounds?'

'I breed fish, myself,' the nephew said.

'Yes, go on,' Gerald said. 'You'll enjoy poking around in that lot.'

'Maybe there'll be something,' Amanda said. 'We'll get it home somehow.'

'Ten pounds,' said Gerald, as they crammed the boxes into Amanda's car. 'You've seen the prices you can get for some of this stuff.'

'It may all be rags,' Amanda said. 'And you have to take the petrol into account, don't you. Maybe we ought to have said five.'

'And he might have taken it at that,' said Gerald. 'No, we did all right. With any luck we shouldn't lose by it. It only takes a couple of things.'

He'd seen a new side to Amanda that day; he was used to her only in relation to himself, he had not known how well she could deal with other people. She made them glad to do things for her, this was it. He would not, he thought, have done so well on his own.

It was not rubbish, they discovered when they got it home. Some of it, of course. But the old sisters had thrown nothing away, and there were clothes dating from the early years of the century; they had taken better care of them, too, than they had of the house. Even on a preliminary sorting it was easy to see that there was enough there to be interesting.

'There's some mould here, look,' Amanda said, smoothing out the folds of a petticoat. 'But I should think it'll come out.'

'You're going to be busy,' Gerald said.

'I don't mind. I'm glad it wasn't a wasted journey. I'd have felt awful.'

'It's always worth going for things,' said Gerald. 'Even if you don't get them. Because you get nothing by sitting around.'

'How dreadful though,' she said. 'Those old ladies. What must it have been like for the one that was left?'

'Probably just thought the other one was having a long lie-in,' said Gerald. 'I wouldn't think about it. There's no point. There's enough in life to worry about without that.'

26

The flat smelt of steam and soapsuds; Amanda had spent the whole day washing and ironing, and it seemed to Denny that she had hardly time for him when he called, late in the afternoon.

'This is it, then, is it?' he said. 'Gerald seemed pleased.'

'It was worth going, you see.'

'All right.' He looked at the clothes heaped everywhere, on tables, the backs of chairs, the floor. 'What a mess. It begins to look like our place.'

'It's cleaner, though,' Amanda said.

'Yes,' he agreed. 'We do try, you know, specially since we've had you to impress, but ... Gerald does, anyway, poor love.' He laughed. 'Him and those slugs.'

'Why is that funny?'

'Because they never get to eat all that stuff he puts down for them, that's why. I throw it out when he's not looking.'

'I never heard of anything so childish.'

'What right's he got to kill them? They're not hurting him.'

'That isn't why you do it.'

'Oh well. ... But it is funny, you must admit. ... He's tried everything. He's been round the shops, asking. He can't make it out.' He studied Amanda's expression. 'You don't think it's funny.'

'Of course I don't. Stop doing it.'

'If you say so,' he shrugged, and paused. 'I'll do anything you want, I don't know if you realise that. Only, you've got to tell me, I'm not very good at guessing.' She said nothing, and he went on, 'Aren't you going to knock off for a bit? I've got to go soon.'

She switched the iron off but did not immediately come to sit beside him as he had hoped she would. 'Look at this,' she said, taking something from a freshly ironed pile of clothes and unfolding it for him to see: 'Isn't it lovely?'

'Oh yes,' he said, not really looking, 'What is it?'

'A christening robe,' she said. 'If it was theirs, and I should think it must be, they weren't married, it must be a hundred years old, nearly. It's all handsewn, look at all those little tucks, and the buttons, they're pearl ... and yards of lace.' She held it up against her: it was so long that it reached almost to her feet.

'People went blind doing that kind of work,' Denny said. 'It's a waste though isn't it really? Baby only wears it five minutes.'

'They're handed down,' Amanda said. 'More than one baby

wears it. It might be even more than a hundred years old. Don't you think it's beautiful?'

'I can't get worked up about things like that,' Denny said. 'Not about anything really. ...' Amanda began to fold the robe, carefully, with sheets of tissue paper between each layer. 'Except that silver dish. That really was beautiful. I wish you'd seen it. Oh yes, I was going to tell you: Mrs Tribe died.'

'Oh no,' said Amanda.

'Well, ninety-three, you can't complain, can you?'

'I know,' Amanda said. 'But it seems so sad, all alone. ...'

'Yes, but isn't everybody? Then, I mean. ... It was all right. She died in her sleep, better than being messed about in hospital don't you think? Anyway she wasn't all that alone, you know what I found out? She'd got this neighbour used to come in every day to see her, make sure she was okay, did a bit of shopping for her and that. All the time she went on about not seeing anyone, wasn't true at all, ungrateful old cow.'

'She was grateful,' said Amanda. 'I'm sure she must have been. She appreciated you going to see her. That's probably why she said that. So you'd feel she appreciated it.'

'What I like about you, you've got such a nice nature,' Denny said. 'No, honestly, I really mean that. This neighbour, she was quite a young girl, with kids, I could tell she was suspicious of me, you know? Must've thought I'd been conning the old girl out of her pension or something.' He laughed. 'It's only the old ladies who trust me.'

'I'm not old,' said Amanda.

'Oh, you,' he said. 'You love me, which isn't quite the same thing. And then again, I don't suppose you really do trust me.' He looked at her as though he expected her to say something; when she didn't, he went on, 'What are you going to do with all this stuff then?'

'Sell it,' said Amanda.

'Yes. Suppose you are ... Gerald's still said nothing to me you know.'

'We've seen one or two possible places. Nothing's definite.'

'Yet.'

'Yet,' agreed Amanda. She had taken out a needle and thread

and was mending the lace frill of a petticoat with careful stitches.

'I reckon he ought to tell me, don't you?' Denny asked. Amanda looked up at him and then bent her head over her work again. 'What about me, then?' Denny went on.

'What about you?'

'What am I supposed to do?'

'I don't know,' she said. She finished off the sewing and snipped the thread. 'This is a ridiculous situation.'

'It does have its amusing moments, yes.'

'I don't mean that. I mean it just can't go on. You've got to tell Gerald.'

'He's your brother. You tell him.'

'I wouldn't ever have made a secret of it. Anyway, you said. ...'

'What did I say?'

'Whatever I wanted, you'd do it.' She was rethreading her needle, her eyes narrowed with concentration.

'Yes, well,' said Denny. 'One says these things ... I meant it though.' He watched her face cloud with disbelief, and added, with a kind of triumph, 'You see, you don't trust me. Do you?'

'Well. ...' said Amanda.

'All right, what do I tell him?'

'I don't know.'

'There you are, then.' He looked at his watch. 'I've got to go in a minute. Come here, will you? You can get on with that when I've gone.' She folded up her work with a precision which irritated him, and sat beside him. He wrapped his arms around her and leaned his head on her shoulder. 'I think you could be making a mistake. About Gerald.'

'What do you mean?'

'If he was going to get anywhere he'd be there by now.'

'He hasn't done badly,' Amanda said. 'From nothing. ...'

'Your father started from nothing and look where he got.'

'Not everybody can be like him.'

'No,' said Denny. 'I don't think Gerald's got it in him. Ideas, that's all he's got. Dreams. He'll never get it together. Look – he's thirty-nine years old and he's barely making a living. If he paid me anything like a decent wage he wouldn't even be doing that.'

'I don't think you're much help to him,' Amanda said.

'I bloody well am. I do more than he does.'

'I mean, support.'

'I just do what I'm told.' He moved his hand across her hair. 'It isn't my business to be supporting.'

'No. It's mine, though.'

'You reckon?' – his mouth moving against her cheek. 'What about me?'

'I don't know what you want,' she said. 'You haven't told me.'

'I'll let you know. I'd better be going now. One of these days I'll bump into Gerald on the stairs. That'd be funny, wouldn't it?'

'I wish you would,' Amanda said. She felt immensely tired, as though his touch had drawn all the energy from her. For some time after he had gone she sat still, her eyes closed, conscious of nothing but emptiness.

27

One good thing was, Gerald and Amanda seemed to have shelved their holiday plans, for the moment at any rate; though there again, it didn't make a whole lot of difference, Denny thought, since Amanda was so busy now that his chances of a moment alone with her were getting smaller all the time; she might almost as well have been in Spain or Africa or one of those places. She was off on her own to sales now, buying clothes; and when she was home she was washing and mending, and Gerald was over there at all hours of the day, admiring the things she'd found, and, no doubt, talking of the future.

'What's she going to do with all that stuff she's buying?'

Denny asked. He was looking forward to hearing Gerald's explanation.

'Well ...,' said Gerald. Now seemed as good a time as any, he supposed. 'Remember, I told you we'd been talking about my ideas? And she was quite interested?'

'What?' said Denny, with a pretence of searching through his mind. 'Oh yes, you did say. ... Only as I never heard anything more about it I thought she must have gone off it or something.'

'No,' said Gerald. 'The reverse, in fact.'

'I wouldn't have thought,' said Denny (laughing inwardly at Gerald, who was obviously feeling uncomfortable about all this) 'that she could manage on her own. I'd have thought she'd need help.'

'Well, yes,' said Gerald.

'Are you trying to tell me something, I wonder?'

'Oh well,' said Gerald. 'Yes. We've got it more or less fixed that we're going to go into it together. There wasn't,' he added quickly, 'much point in saying anything about it up till now. Because it was all up in the air still, you know?'

'And it isn't now, is that it?'

'Not so much.' Gerald couldn't fathom out how Denny was taking this; he was being very cool about it, perhaps he hadn't got the message? 'Of course it'll take a bit of time, I mean, nothing's going to happen overnight, but I thought if you knew about it now you could, well, kind of be prepared.'

'What for, exactly?' Denny asked in feigned perplexity.

'Well, you know,' said Gerald unhappily; this wasn't as easy as he'd thought it would be, 'you could start looking round. ...'

'You would seem to be implying,' said Denny, thoughtful, 'you aren't going to want me much longer. Is that it? or am I jumping to conclusions?'

'Look, I'm sorry –' Gerald began.

'Oh, it's all right,' said Denny.

'It just seemed to me it might be better –'

'Better, oh yes,' said Denny. 'Your idea or hers?'

'Mine I suppose,' said Gerald. 'But she –'

'You're probably right.'

'You think so?' Gerald was relieved. 'Well, I'm glad you feel that way about it.'

'If you really want to know I'm bored out of my mind here,' Denny said, with a fury that surprised both Gerald and himself. 'I'll start looking, don't you worry.'

'Not right away, of course, I don't mean,' Gerald said hastily. He wished he knew where he was with Denny these days.

'Oh well, keep me informed, will you? – I do wonder, though, how long it would have taken you to get around to telling me about all this if I hadn't asked.'

'As a matter of fact Amanda was saying just last night we ought to.'

'Bully for her, then,' Denny said carelessly, and thought, *she's been on at me to tell you something too but I'm buggered if I will just now.* He was surprised (since he had for weeks been expecting what he had just heard) to discover in himself feelings of anger and shock, an almost physical pain, as though Gerald's words had been a knife that cut deep through muscle and nerves. He thought, *if he hadn't been so off-hand about it, if he'd 've said more ... he owes me an explanation at least, doesn't he?* and (salving the hurt, or trying to) *Christ, as if I wanted to stay on anyway. ...*

Later, when Gerald was elsewhere, he went up to his room and took out the *I Ching* and the coins, but his mood was wrong: he could give nothing of himself. He had no patience with the answers that he got, which seemed to him today to be more than usually obscure, wilfully so, enveloped in a meaningless symbolism of water, mountains, fire. The commentaries on the hexagrams were no more than truisms, cracker mottoes. He cast the coins again and again, but each time he turned to the texts his mind clamped shut.

He was on the point of giving it up as a bad job, but he thought he'd let it have one more chance to tell him something worth knowing. He cast the coins unceremoniously, with no proper question formed in his mind, only a truculent kind of general defiance. He opened the book and read: *Let the principal party ... examine himself as if by divination, whether his virtue be great and unremitting and firm. If it be so there will be no error ... we see one seeking union and attachment without having taken the first step to such an end. There will be evil.*

All right, he said as he put the coins away. *All right. You win*; with grudging admiration, for he realised he ought to have known the Book would get at him, sooner or later. That was the creepy thing about it. It didn't ever let you play with it. It would stand so much, but if you weren't prepared to take it seriously, give your mind to it, it turned on you. It had as good as told him that he was wasting his time, not to mention its, by approaching it in a state of mental confusion and anger.

He was tired, anyway, by now, and glad of the excuse to stop.

28

Whenever possible, Denny avoided being around when Amanda came; the less they were all three together, the better, he felt. Today, though, he wanted to be there, because it had been almost a week since he had had a chance to see her. The lack of her parched him: a day was bad enough, this was intolerable.

Amanda and Gerald spent a long time in the yard. Denny watched them through the kitchen window. He could not hear what they were saying. Presently he saw Gerald fetch tools from the van, and open up the bonnet of Amanda's car.

'What's he playing at?' he asked above his thudding heartbeat as she came in.

'It was making rather a strange noise on the way over. He's having a look at it. And I think there's something wrong with the brakes.'

'I wouldn't let him within a mile of it if I was you. He's bloody useless.'

'He seems to know what he's doing.'

'Oh, he's all right at *looking* as if he knows what he's doing. You ought to have asked me.'

'How could I have?'

'Oh well,' said Denny. 'It keeps him happy I suppose. But for Christ's sake get it to a garage after he's been mucking about with it. – He's given me the push, by the way, did you know?'

'Of course I know,' said Amanda.

'Yes, you would. Well?'

'I don't think there's anything to say about it. Is there?'

'Not a lot, no.' Denny took another look at Gerald, bent over the car, and then he caught hold of Amanda and pushed her towards the back door, where there was no possibility of Gerald seeing them. 'I've missed you,' he said.

'Don't –' She tried to move away; he leaned against her, pinning her between himself and the door.

'Have you missed me?'

'Gerald might –'

'He's having a lovely time out there, he won't see us, he can't. Have you?'

'What?'

'Missed me?'

'Please –' she raised an arm to push him away, but he caught her hands and held them.

'You haven't, have you. You don't. Not when you're with Gerald.' There was a loud clanging sound from the yard; Amanda moved, startled, and sent tremors through him. 'Listen, he's dropped a spanner inside it. I bet it makes funnier noises going home than it did coming.'

'Why are you like this about him?'

'I'm not. Like what?' He began to kiss her; she turned her face away.

'You're only doing that' – despairingly – 'because you think it will annoy him. Even if he doesn't know. You like thinking how it would annoy him if he did know.'

'Oh yes?' said Denny, as though he had not really heard her, or was not interested in what she had said. He pressed closer to her; his knees forced themselves between hers. She opened her mouth to protest and his tongue invaded it immediately, quick and slippery as a snake. She did not try to move, was not sure in any case she could, and not only because he held her. The thought that it was the circumstances and not her that excited him, that he was using her as accessory to a private fantasy, appalled and humiliated her, though less so than the hot hollow ache that grew inside her as he rubbed his body against hers. Quite suddenly he pulled away from her, and she could not prevent an involuntary movement towards him; but he held her at arms' length, and the blank look she saw on his face made her feel he thought the whole thing tedious. 'Of course,' he said, 'if you really loved me you'd have told him by now.'

The sound of Gerald's footsteps approaching the door made it impossible for her to speak, even if she could have found the words. Denny did not release his hold on her until it was almost too late: just soon enough for them to move away from the door and from each other. Gerald, coming into the kitchen, had, for no reason that he could put a name to, the sensation of having walked accidentally into an invisible glass door: the same bewildered shock, the shards falling to the ground around him.

29

Suspicion was a malignant growth, developing at lightning speed, making monsters. Until that moment it had not occurred to Gerald that Amanda and Denny could be hiding anything from him; but, now that he had walked unwittingly into a danger zone, everything was contaminated. He turned back in his mind, reviewing words, looks, gestures, and could not now be sure that anything was as it had seemed to be. Sometimes he recoiled from his thoughts, appalled; sometimes he told himself, *I must have been crazy not to have seen it before …*

He said nothing, gave nothing away. *I can hide things too*, he thought. The next evening as he settled down to some paper work, he saw Denny going out, and it was not hard for him to detect a furtive triumph in his departure. Gerald remembered how often Denny's absences coincided with his own staying in. He did not really want to know, and yet he could not hold back from trying to find out. He put aside his papers which were in any case a meaningless confusion to him in his present state, and went out.

The windows of Amanda's flat were dark in the dusk when he arrived there. He rang the bell, expecting no answer, and got none. He walked blindly through the streets, returning again and again to see the same blank mocking windows. On his fourth or fifth – he lost count – circuit he went into a telephone booth and dialled her number. The ringing went on and on until he could no longer stand its jeering staccato laughter and he put the receiver back. He was just pushing the door open when he saw them. They did not see him; they would probably not have recognised him if by chance one or the other had glanced in his direction, they appeared to him so utterly absorbed in one another. After a moment he followed them, at a distance, but close enough to see Denny's hand reach out and hold Amanda's.

He stood still as they approached the door, expecting them to disappear. He did not have the least idea what he would do then. But they stopped too. They were shadows now to him, nothing more, except that Amanda's hair shone faintly in the light from a street lamp, for a while at least, until Denny moved closer to her and the two shadows became one. Gerald remembered that he had once seen his mother leaning against a wall in the dark outside, half-hidden from him by the black anonymous shape of a man, nothing visible of her but her hands clutching the man's buttocks, her splayed legs. – The memory superimposed itself on what he now saw, and fed his anger.

It was not long, although to Gerald it seemed so, before they parted and were lost to him. He waited until Denny had vanished around the street corner and the lights went on in Amanda's flat. He crossed the street with some idea of finding and confronting her, but could not after all raise the courage to do it. He walked, instead, for many hours. His rage did not evaporate in the cool night air, but burnt into a dense mass, a black hole inside him that drew everything into it. By the time he reached home it was late and all was dark and silent, Denny long since returned and no doubt asleep. Gerald was glad of this. He was exhausted and no longer knew what he would have said to him although he had thought about it constantly.

Earlier that evening, Denny had said, 'I'm sorry about yesterday.'

'I don't want to talk about it,' said Amanda. 'I was just going out.'

'Where?'

'Just out. I want some fresh air. I've been in all day.'

'Can I come with you?'

'If you like,' – not encouragingly.

They walked in silence at first. Amanda would not speak and Denny did not dare to, she seemed so distant and unapproachable, and hardly conscious of him beside her. At last, he ventured, 'I suppose I behaved pretty badly.'

'You could say that.'

'Well, I have said it, haven't I? And I said I was sorry.' He began to sound aggrieved, as though his admission had been handsome enough to be rewarded with a warmer response.

'And I said don't talk about it.' Amanda felt her face growing hot and she spoke with her head turned away from him, although twilight had settled around them as they walked and he would probably have noticed nothing.

'I won't then. I just wanted to say though, you were right.'

'What about?'

'Well ... it was because of Gerald, I suppose. I mean, I did get a kick out of thinking he was there, and didn't know.'

She realised then how much she would have liked to be wrong about that. 'Why,' – it wasn't, really, what she most wanted to ask, but all she could, at the moment, manage, 'do you dislike him so?'

'I don't know. I don't, actually, I don't think.'

'What has he done?'

'Nothing.'

'I don't understand –'

'You think I do?'

There seemed to her no point now in not asking, 'Then that's all it is?'

'All what?'

'That's why you –' but she could not say it, and instead, 'why you've been seeing me?'

'I don't know how you can say that,' – surprised and hurt; but how could he have expected her not to ask it?

'Because that's what it seems like.' She took such care to keep emotion from colouring her voice that it sounded, to her, and even more to Denny, hard and cold: words sharp as icicles.

'Don't you believe I love you?'

'I don't really know what you mean by love,' she said. 'No. I don't think you do.'

'What have I got to do to make you believe me?'

'Oh … does it matter?'

'Well, of course it matters. It does to me. Doesn't it to you?'

'I don't know.'

'Listen,' he said. 'If I tell Gerald?'

'You said before you'd tell him. You never did.'

'I mean it this time. Well? If I do?'

'I don't know,' she said again.

'I will, I promise,' and she did not believe him but when he reached for her hand she let him take it.

They were at the door. Denny said, not a question, 'You don't want me to come up.'

'I can't go on like this,' she said miserably.

He put his arms around her, and for a moment, as he held her closely, she wanted very much to think that this was something that concerned the two of them only, but she could not drive from her mind the thought that Denny had, buried not all that deeply in his, an image of Gerald: that this scene was being played for an audience of one, whose back was turned but who might at any second glance in their direction. Beyond Denny, across the street, she saw, or it seemed to her that she saw, a motionless figure, whether watching them or not it was impossible to tell, now that it had grown so dark; but the idea that they might be seen, and, too, the response that her body, of its own accord and against the urgent promptings of her reason, made to Denny's nearness, were enough for her to draw back; sensing, as she did, to her dismay, a physical disappointment that he could let his arms slide so easily from her and make no attempt to stop her going.

'I don't,' he said hesitantly, 'want to lose you.'

One says these things, she thought as she turned and went wordlessly indoors.

He waited until she had quite disappeared before he himself began to move slowly away. She had frightened him badly. He had no idea of the uncertainties that troubled her; he had tonight seen in her only a new determination that chilled him through and through. He had no difficulty in believing that she meant what she said. All the way home he nerved himself for his encounter with Gerald; when he arrived it was by no means a relief to find that the words he had prepared so carefully could not after all be spoken yet. He took out his coins: he felt as much in need of guidance as he had ever done, and he was sure that tonight he was in the proper frame of mind to deal patiently with whatever he might be told. '... *the possession of sincerity, through which the mind is penetrating*,' he read, and was encouraged; but then, looking further, he saw, '... *whether he comes or goes, confronted by a defile. All is peril to him and unrest. (His endeavours) will lead him into the cavern of the pit.* ...' He felt betrayed. There was no all-seeing and impartial genius in the Book; a warped malicious demon, possibly, or, more likely, nothing: as well trust the whirling drums of a fruit machine to deliver valuable wisdom. *How can you tell me that*, he said, disgusted, and slung the book away. He felt his resolve begin to curdle, and he blamed Gerald for staying out so unusually late. When, later still, he heard Gerald at last come in, he was near enough to sleep to be able to persuade himself easily that he had nothing to say that could not be better said the next day.

30

The next morning, though, he wished he'd had, or made, the chance the night before, when he was keyed up to speak. Gerald seemed moody and preoccupied, there was a lot to do, the time was never right: he let it go. But now and then he was struck cold by the thought that Amanda had been in earnest when she said she could not, would not go on; and he wanted to say it and get it over with, if only Gerald's face had not worn that barricaded look.

Late afternoon, he had a delivery to make. When he had got the van loaded up, he went in to fetch the keys. Gerald was sitting in the kitchen, staring emptily.

'I'm off,' Denny said. 'You going out, later?'

'I saw you,' said Gerald.

'You what?'

'Last night,' said Gerald. 'I saw you.' He too had spent the day in indecision, and more tormentedly. His choice lay between hearing the truth from Amanda and hearing it from Denny, and he had not, until now, been able to make up his mind which would be worse; but he knew, suddenly, that he could not face Amanda again without a clearer picture of her betrayal of him.

'Oh, well,' said Denny. He sat down opposite Gerald. There wasn't any doubt of Gerald's meaning: he had only to look at him. He wondered now why he had not realised sooner the reason for his blank glaring face. 'We were going to tell you, anyway. I was going to tell you.'

'What were you going to say?' Gerald's eyes looked through a mask; Denny would have preferred anger, he would at least have had some idea how to respond to him.

'Well ... it's obvious, isn't it?'

'It's obvious, all right,' said Gerald. He continued to stare and Denny grew uneasy. He could not go on looking at him; he began to tug at a splinter on the edge of the table.

'Well, that's it, really, isn't it,' he said vaguely.

'You've told me nothing,' said Gerald.

'I don't know what you want to know.'

Gerald got to his feet so abruptly that his chair went skittering across the floor; he steadied it, gripping the back tightly with both hands. His knuckles were pale. 'Everything,' he said. 'I want to know everything. You owe it to me.'

'Don't owe you a thing,' said Denny, more confident now he had a reaction to play against. ' 'S nothing at all to do with you really, is it?'

Gerald had promised himself he would not lose his temper, whatever happened; there wasn't anything to be gained by it. He had thought that he could remain in control of himself; but Denny could hardly, if he'd tried, have said anything more likely to make him forget that promise. He did not lift the chair and throw it, nor did he shout and rage, but a stretched string broke somewhere in his mind. He said tonelessly, aware of the banality of the question, 'How long has it been going on?'

'Oh well,' said Denny. 'Right from the beginning, really.'

'She never told me anything,' said Gerald. He was talking to himself but there was no way Denny could know this.

'I told her you wouldn't like it.'

'Like it?' said Gerald. 'You expect me to like it?'

'No,' Denny said, impatiently. 'I told you, I knew you wouldn't.'

'Why her?' said Gerald. 'That's the thing ... why her?'

'I didn't choose,' said Denny.

Gerald said, 'It made me feel sick, last night, watching you.'

'Come on, you must've had some idea,' said Denny, thinking it over, 'you're not telling me you just happened to be there.'

'Sick,' repeated Gerald.

'See,' Denny said. 'I knew you wouldn't like it.'

'Nobody,' said Gerald – generalities were less painful – 'likes to see someone mucking about with their sister.'

'Mucking about. Come off it.'

'I saw you.'

'Oh well,' said Denny. 'Don't you kiss her?'

'That's different. She's my sister. Not like that.'

'Maybe you'd like to,' said Denny.

'What did you say?'

'You're not telling me, are you,' Denny said slowly, 'that it's normal to get so worked up about what your sister does?'

'Normal?' echoed Gerald. His brain snatched at the words, tore them to pieces, sucked out the meaning. 'That's disgusting, what you're saying.'

'Oh, I don't know,' said Denny. 'Just because I never wanted to screw my sister's no reason why you –'

'You're filthy,' said Gerald.

'I don't see what's so wrong with it, myself.' It had never before occurred to Denny to speculate on the nature of Gerald's feelings for Amanda. Now that he had he found the idea pathetic, perhaps, certainly not repellent; he was touched, and felt for the first time something like remorse for the way he had deceived Gerald. He looked at him: he was leaning with both hands on the table, as though his own weight had suddenly grown too much for him to bear. Denny felt himself moved, ridiculously, almost to tears. He imagined that he had won in whatever conflict there had been between them; having hurt Gerald, he could afford to be generous. He said, 'You know, I like you. I thought I didn't but I think I do after all.'

Gerald scarcely heard this, and if he had it would have seemed entirely irrelevant to him. He was too occupied with his own thoughts for anything else to penetrate his mind. After a moment he said, painfully, 'Have you, you and her, have you. ...'

'Have we what?'

Gerald could not say it. The thought was bad enough; the words were impossible. He could only stare his meaning.

'Oh that,' said Denny. 'No. As a matter of fact, no, actually. ...' The question embarrassed him and made his denial sound unconvincing.

'I don't believe you,' said Gerald.

'Oh Christ,' said Denny, 'I tell you, we haven't ... what's it matter anyway?'

'Matter?'

'You want her to save it for you, is that it?'

'Get out,' said Gerald. He was incoherent with rage; words stuck in his throat like rising vomit. 'Filth –'

'Just because you're so bloody hung-up –'

'I don't want to hear –'

'Doesn't mean everyone else's got to –'

'I said get out.'

'All right, I'm going,' said Denny. He picked up the keys,

hesitated. 'I wish you'd believe me though.'

'As if I could believe anything you ...,' said Gerald. 'I know you.' Denny shrugged, and started for the door. 'Things,' Gerald said, 'there's things she ought to know about you.'

'Yeah?' said Denny, not turning.

'She mightn't like ...'

'She knows,' said Denny.

'Everything?'

'Most.' He faced Gerald. 'But if you tell her anything I'll fucking well kill you.' Gerald sat, hearing the van door slam, the engine roar. When he was sure that Denny had gone, he got up and went out. He ran to the station, bumping into people in his haste – not noticing. He could not hope that Denny was not now on his way to see Amanda, but with any luck the traffic at this time of day would hold him up enough for Gerald to get there first.

31

He did not know what he was going to say to Amanda, only that he had to see her, though as he approached her door, he was sickened, and thought that it almost might be better if he never saw her again. He did not want lies from her, he did not want the truth, if the truth was what he thought. Nothing she could say now would make things as they had been, as he had supposed them to be. Denny had said too much. He did, however, ring the bell; he was not strong enough to turn and walk away.

He had no need to speak when he saw her; his face spoke for him. 'He's told you,' Amanda said.

'Yes. He's told me.'

'I'm sorry.'

'Yes.' He felt suddenly, immensely, unbearably tired. He pushed past her and sat down, his face in his hands. She followed him and sat beside him.

'Gerald,' she said. He did not move or give any sign that he heard her. She touched his shoulder, tentatively; he flinched. 'I'm glad you know,' she said, and laughed, unsurely. 'It's strange, it seems all of a sudden like some kind of bad dream. Like another person ... I don't know, now, how I can possibly not have told you. ...'

'I don't know either,' he said. 'A bad dream? I wish it was.' He looked at her. Her face was so open that it hurt him, much more than guilt would have done. 'Perhaps you were ashamed to tell me.'

'I'm ashamed I didn't tell you,' she said, not understanding.

'Nothing else?'

'No. ...'

'You don't sound sure.'

'I am sure,' she said.

'I think I'd better go now,' he said. 'It was a mistake to come.'

'Don't go. Not while you're angry.'

'Seeing you makes me angry,' he said, 'and thinking of you and him –' he couldn't finish.

'What?'

'I don't know what word you use,' he said. 'Screwing, is how Denny puts it.' Funny how he could say it after all, as though it didn't matter any more.

It took Amanda several seconds to realise what he meant. 'No,' she said. 'He didn't tell you that.'

'He did.' At that moment, Gerald honestly believed Denny's denial to have been admission; but when he looked at her bewildered face, he knew that he had been wrong. He knew too that he had a better weapon against Denny than he could have imagined.

'But he couldn't have. It's not true. ...'

'In great detail.' Gerald watched her closely and saw revulsion creep into her expression. He shook his head. 'I don't like that kind of talk at the best of times, but when it's about you. ...'

'It isn't true,' she said desperately.

'I know,' he assured her gently, 'now I've seen you, I know, I believe you. ... Maybe I shouldn't have believed him when he said it, but what was I to think? I knew there was something, Amanda, I'm not stupid. ...'

'Why did he tell you that?'

'I don't know.' Gerald thought a little. 'To hurt me? He'd know it would.'

'Yes,' she said, and he was delighted that she accepted his explanation so easily.

'The truth is, you know, he envies us. Has done, right from the beginning. I said as much, didn't I? Remember?' Amanda nodded. 'Well then. That's why.'

Amanda sat motionless. What Gerald was telling her was all too believable. Everything that had taken place between her and Denny seemed to bear it out: his insistence on keeping it all secret, his constant digs at Gerald, his behaviour the other day, when it should have been clear to her, had been clear, that what interested him in their relationship was not her but its hypothetical effect on Gerald. It was no wonder to her now that he had never been concerned with the future, had made no plans, had wanted nothing from her except lukewarm passionless embraces, necessary for the game that he was playing. She tried to think of him and could remember nothing: not his face or the sound of his voice or even her own feelings. It was as though a sponge had passed across the surface of her memory, obliterating everything that had to do with him.

Gerald was saying, '– of course, it could have been ... I mean, did he want you to, did he try. ...'

'No,' said Amanda dully, 'no, nothing like that.'

Gerald could not have been happier or more full of relief at the way things were turning out if Amanda had been kidnapped and he, fearing her death or mutilation, had instead had her returned to him without ransom, unharmed, unchanged. He had had images in his mind of Denny's hands moving over her body, leaving a trail, shining obscenely, like the ones the slugs made, and now he looked at her and saw that nothing had touched her. He slipped his arm around her and drew her head on to his shoulder. Presently he became aware that she was crying. He was not distressed; it pleased him, rather, that he was there to comfort her, and he rocked her gently and let her go on crying; until the doorbell rang, jarringly, and he felt her tense against him and hold back her tears, listening.

'Let it ring,' he said.

'But –'

'You know who it'll be. He'll go away.' The bell rang many times.

Amanda scarcely seemed to breathe. 'There's no point, is there,' Gerald said. 'You can't want to see him?'

Amanda shook her head. 'But he isn't going away.'

Gerald said, 'He will.'

Indeed, after five minutes or so, the bell stopped ringing. Amanda sat up straight and rubbed the drying tears from her face; she had been startled out of her need to cry. 'Shall I make you something?' Gerald said. 'Tea, coffee?'

'I will,' she said, but he had already got up. She followed him into the kitchen, as though she felt protected by the sight of him.

'If he comes back –' she said.

'You don't ever have to see him,' Gerald said. 'I'll have it out with him tonight, when I get back. After the things he said to me, I don't want him around any more either.' He foresaw problems with Denny, but he put off thinking about them for the time being.

The telephone started to ring. When it had rung fifteen or twenty times, Amanda said, distraught, 'I can't bear it.'

'Don't answer it.'

'I'm not going to. But –'

'He'll give up in time.' *He'll try again though and I won't always be here.* ... The ringing stopped, and began again almost immediately. Amanda moved towards the living room; Gerald caught hold of her. His hands gripped her more tightly than Denny's ever had. 'You won't have to speak to him again, ever,' he said. He held her until at last there was silence, then he went quickly into the next room and took the receiver off the hook. 'There,' he said. 'You'll have peace tonight at any rate.' He felt pleasure at the thought that Denny was now tasting some of the torment that he had known the previous evening.

Amanda did not think it peace, even though the telephone was quiet and the doorbell did not ring again. She felt numb and empty. Gerald poured tea and talked about their plans. It was, he said, all the more important now that they should get going properly. There was nothing holding them back. 'It will be a new life for both of us, Amanda,' he told her. 'It's what we need. You'll see, you'll forget about him before long. ...' She listened with half her mind and filled the spaces between his words with murmurs of agreement, though there seemed little meaning to her in what he was saying.

It grew very late; reluctantly, Gerald decided that it was time for him to go. It was no use pretending that Denny didn't exist (though how pleasant it would have been if that had been so.) He had to be dealt with, and the sooner the better. 'Leave the phone off,' he told her. 'Ring me in the morning.' He leaned over her. 'We don't need anyone else, do we?' He kissed her, and she flung her arms around him and moved her head so that his lips, instead of brushing her cheek, were pressed against hers. He was disturbed, and said, as soon as he was able, 'Amanda, he said terrible things, about you and me. ... It isn't like that, it isn't necessary, all that ...' and Amanda, who had felt her misery eased during the brief moment that their mouths had touched, was overwhelmed by an even greater confusion and despair.

32

At first, Denny was certain that Gerald was wholly to blame for Amanda's refusal to see him. It was easier to think that; it filled his mind with anger and left no room for anything else. Little by little, though, as the hours went emptily by and Gerald did not return, and all he heard when he dialled Amanda's number was a single note, repeated endlessly, a colder idea crept into his mind. He could not help remembering how remote from him

Amanda had seemed the evening before, how unmoved by anything he had said. It could be, and the more he thought about it the more he began to fear that it was, simply that she had after all had enough. His memories gave him no comfort; there was nothing that she had ever said or done that he could use now to persuade himself that she loved him. The protestations and promises, such as they were, had all been his. *Peril and unrest ... the cavern of the pit ...* was this what it had meant, then, that nothing he did would change the stark fact that she was lost to him? His mind gnawed the thought ceaselessly, rubbing itself raw on it.

He was so deep in his own inner labyrinth that it was a shock to hear Gerald at the door, and he scarcely knew what he could say to him. Gerald entered, wary and alert, like someone who suspects an ambush ahead. For a moment neither of them spoke. Then Denny burst out: 'What did you tell her?'

'Nothing,' said Gerald.

'You were there, weren't you? What did you say?'

'I didn't have to say anything.'

'What do you mean? You must have. She won't talk to me.'

'No,' said Gerald. 'She doesn't want to.'

'Why?'

'She just doesn't.'

'I don't believe you.'

'Well,' said Gerald. 'You've seen, haven't you. She doesn't.'

'At least she'll have told you you were wrong, what you thought.'

'Oh yes,' said Gerald. 'She did.'

'What else did she say?'

'She doesn't want to see you any more, that's all.'

'She must have said why.'

'Work it out for yourself,' said Gerald. He had no intention of letting himself be pushed into saying too much. 'I'm tired. I'm going to bed.' He moved towards the stairs.

'I'll find out, you know,' said Denny. 'If you're telling the truth or not.'

Gerald paused on the bottom step. 'Okay,' he said. 'You find out. If you can,' – and continued up the stairs, half-expecting to hear Denny's voice pursuing him; but, to his great relief, he seemed, for the moment at least, to have silenced him. What to do in the morning, he hoped his sleeping mind might discover.

Denny tried the phone once more, after Gerald had gone. The ringing tone was so unexpected that his heart sprang startled and beat against the bars of its cage; but there was time enough for it to grow calm again, as he hung on, listening, time enough to waken even the soundest sleeper. He held the receiver closely, as though he could force feeling through the wires, long after any hope he'd had of being answered had seeped away from him.

33

Gerald was up early the next morning, long before Denny was stirring, and he was still alone downstairs when at eight o'clock the phone rang. He answered it immediately, anxious not to be overheard.

'Gerald?' said Amanda's voice; faint, as though she were whispering.

'Yes. – Can you hear me?' he asked, when she said nothing.

'Yes.'

'Listen, I don't expect there'll be any trouble. I think Denny realises, you know, I think he'll leave you alone,' said Gerald with a confidence he did not in fact feel.

'Did he say anything?'

'Not a lot.'

'Oh.'

'I'll be over as soon as I can get away.'

'I'm not at the flat.'

'Where are you?'

'I'm in Wales. At the cottage. You remember –'

'You're where?'

'I couldn't sleep last night. I didn't know what to do. I drove down, I've just got here.'

'There wasn't any need –'

'I want to be on my own for a few days.'

'Why on your own?'

'I want to think.'

'What about, Amanda? You're not going to change your mind about ... about anything?'

'No, you mustn't think that. But I do want to be alone.'

'All right. But –'

'Just a day or two.'

'Can I come down, when you've had enough of being on your own? I'd like –'

'Maybe. I don't know how I'll feel. I might come straight back tomorrow, the next day, it depends. ...'

'Perhaps it's a good idea anyway. In case he tries. ... Yes, it's the best thing you could have done, really. ... You'll ring me, every day?'

'Of course I will.'

'Or you could give me your number, I'll ring you. He might –'

'Gerald, please understand. I don't want you to ring me. Not for the moment. If I want to get in touch with you I will.' He had never heard such firmness in her voice; he could not argue with it.

'If I promise I won't try to ring or anything, will you tell me where you are, I mean, exactly? I can't stand not knowing where you are.'

'All right.' She spelt out the unfamiliar Welsh place-names for him, and he repeated them after her as he scribbled them down.

'I feel better, knowing,' he said.

The kitchen lino was cold under Denny's bare feet as he stood with his ear pressed to the crack of the door. He thought he'd better go now. He didn't want to leave Gerald talking to her and not know what was being said, but neither did he want to be discovered listening; besides, he was carrying in his mind, carefully and precariously, like a tray of brimming glasses, the address he'd heard Gerald repeating; he needed to write it down before it spilled over into meaninglessness. He crept across the kitchen; the sheet he'd wrapped round him toga-like when the ringing phone had startled him awake and out of bed trailed behind him on the floor with a soft shushing sound louder than his footfalls. He was at the door of his room before he heard the phone being put down. He found a stub of pencil, picked at the wood around the lead to get enough point to write with, and set down on a scrap of paper what he remembered. From a pile of books he took out an atlas, and sitting crosslegged on his bed he studied the map of Wales. It took him some time to find what he was looking for. In the middle of his search he heard Gerald coming upstairs; he froze. Gerald spoke his name, quietly. Denny held his breath until the footsteps started downstairs again. Then he returned to the map. He found more paper and copied out a rough route-plan. Gerald was out in the yard now, banging about inside the van. Denny dressed. He turned out his pockets; he had four pounds and some loose change. All his other money was in the safe, and Gerald had the key, so it was going to have to do. He went cautiously downstairs, slipped the bolts on the shop door, and set out for the station. He aimed to get a little way out of London before he started hitching.

When, later, Gerald discovered he'd gone he wasn't all that surprised. He imagined him hanging about near Amanda's flat in the hope of seeing her: the thought amused him. He was glad after all she'd had the idea to get away for a bit: it would give him time to sort things out with Denny.

34

Amanda was tired; an immense, overwhelming tiredness that kept her where she was, too weary for the effort of going to bed. It had been impossible to sleep the night before; thoughts had padded obsessively to and fro inside her brain, going nowhere. She thought of Gerald, she thought of Denny; her feelings twisted and knotted themselves inextricably. The drive in the darkness had deadened her mind. She had thought that she might sleep when she arrived at the cottage, and wake to greater clarity, but she hadn't been able to; she hadn't felt at all like sleeping. She had gone to see the Thomases at the farm down in the valley, who kept an eye on the cottage, to reassure them that it was her and not vandals up there. She had sat and drunk tea in their kitchen and heard their kind voices talking about her father. Later, she had driven into the nearby town and bought things she supposed she might need. She walked a little. It was colder here than it had been in London; summer had been gone from these hills for some time now. When she got back she lit a fire in the hearth, for comfort as well as for warmth. She tried to read, and found it hard to keep her eyes open, but when she lay back and willed her mind to empty itself, thoughts began to swirl in again, chilly and thick as mountain mist.

It had been a mistake to come here; she knew that already. The place was too full of her father; it reminded her too harshly of the time when her affections had been simple, undivided; it brought home to her how totally she had forgotten him in the last few months. There was nothing in the house that had not been chosen, made, worked on by him. Feelings changed, but things remained unaltered, their steadfastness a reproach to her. *But I couldn't have gone on like that*, she said aloud, her voice falling strangely in the silent room. *So empty and hopeless, you couldn't have wanted that.* The thought that she must in time forget Denny and the pain of loving was no consolation at all; knowing that this misery was ultimately useless, that it would end in nothing, in blankness, emptiness, made it the more unbearable.

On the edge of sleep, she was hurtled into complete waking by the sudden loud sound of knocking at the door. She sat bolt upright, terrified. Her heart jumped wildly. The knocking came again. Mr Thomas would not come up here, so late. They would all be in bed now, and asleep, down there at the farm. She tried to think, through the noise of the knocker and the thudding of her heart, whether she had locked the back door;

whether she should ring for help now, while she had the chance. …

The knocking stopped, and she heard a voice calling her name. She got up and went to the door, and because who else knew that she was there, she said, as soon as there was silence, 'Gerald?'

'It's not Gerald,' said Denny, furious. 'Come on, for Christ's sake, Amanda, let me in.'

She opened the door slowly, letting in the damp night air and Denny, who pushed past her without seeming to see her. He had spent so long thinking of what he would say to her that now he did not want to say anything. His shoulders were streaked with rain. He took his coat off and threw it on the back of a chair.

'I've been on the road fourteen bloody hours, you could at least let me in.' She picked up his coat and hung it up on the door. Looking at her, finally, he saw that she was in her dressing-gown. 'Were you asleep?'

'No.'

'That's all right then.' He went to the fire and warmed himself, then sat down on the floor and began to take off his shoes and socks. He had a blister on one heel and winced with pain as he prised the sock loose from it. 'I had to walk the last bit, there was nothing on the road. What a place to live. No wonder you thought you'd be safe here.'

'Did Gerald tell you where I was?'

'Of course he bloody didn't.'

'Then how –'

'It doesn't matter. What did he say to you?'

'Gerald?'

'Of course, Gerald. What did he say? He must've told you something or you wouldn't have gone off like that.'

'He said –' and stopped. The possibility that Gerald had been lying fell into her mind like a stone. She stared at Denny as though she had never seen him before.

'I know he told you something about me.'

'He said you told him that we, that we had –'

'What?' It was the effort of adjusting to things, if Gerald had not been telling the truth, that made it hard for her to speak; but Denny took it for embarrassment, and saw an answer in her silence. 'You and Gerald are a pair,' he said. 'So fucking uptight, you can't say it. ... That's it, isn't it? He said I'd told him we'd been having it off. Yes?' She nodded. 'Is that all?'

'Yes.'

'And you believed him.' She said nothing. 'I didn't tell him that. You could at least have asked me.'

'I'm sorry.'

'You'd believe anything he told you, I suppose. Well. Do you believe me, now?'

'Yes.' She did; but belief did not make everything immediately easy.

'I wouldn't do that.' He paused. 'I mean I wouldn't have told him that, not if it wasn't true.'

'I know that's what you mean.'

'I want to make love to you of course.' He looked at her and saw no change in her expression; her serious, still faintly alarmed and, it seemed to him, accusing face made him angry. 'It's all right, you know. I'm not going to rape you or anything.'

'Of course not,' she said. 'There wouldn't be any fun in that, would there?'

'I don't know what you're getting at,' he said. 'Anyway. I'm not going, you know. Not tonight. Not after having come all this way.'

'I didn't ask you to go.'

'Make me some tea or something, will you? Only not that rubbish you usually have. You've got Gerald buying it now, you know; he thinks it's elegant. I have to get my own if I want a decent cup of tea.'

'You could have told me before you didn't like it,' she said. 'I'll see what there is. Do you want something to eat?'

'I'm not hungry. I had some chips in some Christ-awful place I can't pronounce the name of. Coffee'll do. Anything.' He got to his feet. 'I suppose there's a bathroom?'

'Through there.' She pointed. 'I had a bath earlier but the water should have warmed up a little by now.'

'I just want to piss.' He was suddenly very strongly aware of the smell of bath oil or talcum powder that hung around her: lemony, a little too sweet, cloying. ... In the bathroom he was overtaken by a spasm of nausea; he leaned over the lavatory bowl and spat out the bitter liquid that filled his mouth. His stomach turned and settled again. He splashed water on his face. Nothing was as he had hoped it would be. He could not think now why he had bothered to come.

'I don't suppose,' he said, drinking the coffee that she had made for him, 'there was a bathroom when sheep farmers or whoever lived here.'

'No,' she said. 'My father put it in.'

'Very nice. There are people living in slums. People with no homes at all. No wonder places like this get set on fire.'

'It had been empty for years before we bought it. No one wanted to live here. It was a shell. He did everything to it himself.'

'I know. You've told me. Never happy unless he was working. Where did it get him, though?'

'He had a good life.'

'Oh sure.'

'I'd rather not talk about him, anyway.'

'Suits me.' He looked at her. She was leaning back in the corner of the couch; her face was pale and pinched with exhaustion. 'Why don't you go to bed?' he said. 'You look terrible.'

'What about you?'

'I'll sleep here. Don't worry about me.'

'I mean. ...' It was at once a test of his feelings for her and a proof of her belief in them, but she was tired and still suffering from the confusion of the last twenty-four hours, and the right words were hard to find, 'you're so angry. I don't want you to be. If it's what you really want ... you said it was. ...' It was not all she had meant to say, but it would have to do.

'Are you inviting me into your bed?' He laughed incredulously. 'Terrific. I don't think so though.' He stared at the fire. 'In the first place, I'm too bloody exhausted.' He watched the flames licking the edges of a glowing lump of coal.

'And as I wasn't expecting such a generous offer I'm not exactly prepared for it. If you know what I mean.' He listened to the soft hiss and crackle from the grate that were the only sounds in the room. 'Anyway,' he said, 'it isn't really all that important, you know. Thanks all the same.'

He swung round to face her, wanting to see whether his words had hurt her enough; and saw immediately that they had: far too much. He could no longer bear anything that was happening. He moved across to her and leaned his head against her thigh. 'I'm sorry,' he said. 'Amanda. I'm sorry.' Her hands touched his hair, his face; her fingers found tears in the corners of his eyes and brushed them away. He had the dizzying sense of things having all at once turned the right way up again. He kept his eyes tightly shut while the world fell into place around him.

Amanda continued to move her hands across his face; her touch was like that of a blind person, creating an image out of darkness.

'Why did you believe what Gerald told you?' he said at last.

'I don't know. It seemed to fit,' she said. 'You never –'

'It would do, I suppose.'

'I thought it did.'

'It's my fault, I know. ... Listen.' He pulled himself up to sit beside her, holding her close, feeling her warmth enter his blood. 'It wasn't the main thing, ever, getting at Gerald, I mean, but ... I knew he wouldn't like it, I knew he couldn't stand sharing you, and it seemed easier, not telling him, and then ... I don't know if you'll understand this ... it was the only way, I thought it was the only way, I could cope with how I felt about you. Making it a kind of game. Do you understand? It made it all less real, somehow.'

'Why didn't you want it to be real?'

'I'm so completely yours it's frightening,' he said. 'I never felt like this. It was too much, I couldn't take it. – You know what I said just now? About sex not being all that important? I wanted to hurt you, I suppose, because, well, because I'm frightened, but it's true too in a way. ... When I think of the things I've done with people who meant nothing to me, who I wouldn't want to spend five minutes talking to – it's easier than talking, you know, a lot of the time, you give less – it makes it meaningless.' He touched her mouth with the tips of his fingers. 'Not just women, you know. There were times I needed money, badly, and you can do anything, with anyone, you know, when it's like that. … It didn't seem to matter all that much.'

'It doesn't matter,' she said.

'No, it doesn't. I thought that might have been what Gerald told you, and you. … Anyway. Of course none of it matters, but it's just because it doesn't that it was hard for me to think of you and me. … So I made it be a game.'

'Not any more though.'

'Not any more.' He looked at their hands resting, fingers interlocked, on his knee. 'It's not just what I want … not just something to make me happy. It has to be both of us. And anyway … Being with you, like this, is almost enough. For the moment. I'm not asking … you know – this sounds a bit funny but you'll understand, I hope you do – this is the first time I've really been happy with you.'

'Yes.'

'You feel like that too?'

'Yes … yes, I do. That's just what it's like.'

'So … it's enough. For now. – Of course,' he said after a while, drowsily and with no urgency, 'I could make you want me, I expect.' He eased his hand from hers and lifted it to touch her neck, then let it move slowly and lightly down her body until it rested in her lap.

'You don't have to do that,' she said.

'No?' He turned his head so that he could look into her eyes. 'Tell me.'

'I want to,' she said. 'I was never sure you did.'

'You know now?'

'Yes.'

'That's good.' His hand returned to hers. 'All the same, though,' he leaned his head on her shoulder, 'not now? I'm tired, aren't you? It'll keep. – I never thought, did you, that things could be so simple, after all.'

'Are they, though?'

'Aren't they?' He lay down with his head in her lap. 'Do you love me because you can't love Gerald, I wonder?'

'I do love Gerald.'

'You know what I mean.'

'Yes,' she said. 'I don't know. Does it matter?'

'I suppose not. – I didn't mean to start talking about Gerald.'

'He still exists, though.'

'Yes.' For once, it didn't seem important. He closed his eyes; he floated. It seemed to him that he was high above the earth, and all its confused shapes were patterns now that shifted and reformed the further he travelled; moons, constellations, galaxies moved unerringly into their places.

Amanda watched his sleeping face and envied him his certainty. She had no doubts left about herself and him, but Gerald refused to be excised from her thoughts. Her mind was too tired to balance everything: the shapes that swam in it were confused and fragmented. After a little she moved, carefully, trying not to disturb Denny; nevertheless he woke. 'Don't go away,' he said.

'I'm still here.' She knelt by the hearth and made up the fire, which had burned low. She turned off the light. The darkness was soft and reassuring; she felt eased, as though the light had held her in too tight a grasp. *When I've slept*, she thought, *I will be able to think more clearly. Things must really be simple, as he says. It's being tired that makes it hard to see* ... She no longer felt torn between Gerald and Denny, as she had previously; there was now no question of that: it was more as though each of them had laid such heavy weights upon her that she was in danger of being crushed.

Denny had moved to make room for her beside him on the couch. She lay down, easing her body to fit against his. 'I wish I could tell you,' he said, 'how much ...' he sighed, and slept. His arm across her grew heavier, the deeper he sank into sleep. It was not long before she ceased to notice it, and the light touch of his breath on her cheek, and his warmth as he pressed close to her.

35

Denny dreamed; and shortly before dawn his dreams woke him, enough for him to know that she was really there; not enough for him to think beyond his desire. Last night, it had been diffused throughout his body, and easily contained; now it had drawn itself into a tight mass in his loins, insistent. He heard the sudden catch in her breath as his hands, gripping hers, drew her out of her sleep. As though he were still the creature of his dreams, and absolved from all responsibility of anything that happened in them, he began to pull at his clothes. 'Please,' he said, 'Amanda, please. ...' It was still too dark for him to see her face with any clearness: he could not tell what she was thinking; not that it mattered much to him in any case, not just now. ... Her hand went with his, unresisting. She said, 'I don't know what you want me to do.' Her fingers moved tentatively. 'I mean, how. ...'

'Show you.'

'Is that right?'

'Yes ...' and said nothing more until his dream burst dazzlingly and he lay among its drifting fading fragments. The shapes of reality grew clearer, alarming him. 'Amanda,' he said; she didn't speak, and he said again, his desperate need now only for reassurance, 'Amanda? I'm sorry, I. ...'

'Why sorry?'

'I didn't give you time to think.'

'How much time,' she said seriously, 'does one need?'

'Oh, I don't know,' he said. 'But all the same.'

'Don't be sorry,' she said. 'I told you. ...'

'No, but,' he said. 'It was selfish. I didn't mean it to be like that.'

'Another time it won't be.'

'No, it won't, I promise. ... Do you still love me?'

'Of course,' she said, puzzled that he should ask that now.

'You don't ever say it. I don't think you ever have.'

'Does it need saying?'

'No.'

'I love you.'

Light was beginning to show dimly at the edges of the curtains. They could see each other now. The fire had burnt down into soft ashes. It was not yet cold in the room but there was already a hint of chill creeping in with the light. Denny sat up, reluctantly, fastening his jeans, tucking his shirt in. 'Well,' he said. 'What do we do now? – I suppose,' feeling he should say it, 'we're going back to London?'

Amanda pulled at the nightdress clinging stickily to her body. 'Yes,' she said. 'We have to. Don't you think so?'

'Yes.' He wished that it were possible to pretend, if only for a little longer, that they could stay and play at desert islands, but he knew it wasn't, and had known before he spoke. 'I can't stay with Gerald, though, can I, not now?'

'No.'

'I'll find somewhere.'

'You might as well stay with me.'

'You sure?'

'Yes.' She touched his face. 'Yes, really.'

In the kitchen, they drank coffee. Neither felt like eating. Amanda had not bothered to unpack the things she had bought the day before; the cardboard box they came in stood on the dresser. She collected together the few things that needed washing, poured the remaining milk down the sink. 'I don't expect I shall be coming here again,' she said, almost to herself. 'I wonder if there's anything I should take?'

'We aren't going to spend our honeymoon here, then?' he asked.

'Are we having one of those?' she said, and because he didn't expect anything like that from her, and she spoke, besides, with such apparent solemnity, it was a moment before he caught the teasing note in her voice, and was disconcerted, though delighted, by it. 'This is so sudden,' she said, laughing at him, almost, he realised, flirting with him: it was nothing like he'd known from her before.

'Oh, well,' he said, 'it'd be nice to have a legal claim.' It was the wrong thing to have said, he knew that at once: her lightheartedness faded. 'I don't mean that,' he said hurriedly. 'I mean, I couldn't ever see the point, but right now it seems the only thing. I know it's ridiculous, but I can't think how else to show how serious I am.' He knew though, and was ashamed, that at the back of his mind there was a need for formal commitment: a proof of ownership.

'If it's what you want,' she said, as though it made no difference to her one way or the other; as indeed it did not. Ridiculous, she might have agreed with him, though not for his reasons, which had to do with facile prejudice against outworn bourgeois institutions, but rather because the question of whether or not they married seemed to her insignificant, not to say irrelevant, against the commitment they already had to one another. Part of her mind was busy with her own thoughts as she listened to him now speaking of the future with an earnestness that she found somehow touching.

'... something,' he was saying. 'I don't know what. But you'll see, I can ... I know I've spent my whole life messing about, but –'

'Whatever we do,' she interrupted; since it had to be said, it might as well be now as later, 'I mean, whatever you and I do, you know I shall still see Gerald?'

'Oh,' he said, taken aback; this had really not occurred to him.

'Oh well, yes. I suppose you must, now and then, but. ...' He thought himself generous, since it cost him an effort to say even this much, and to say it lightly. He found it difficult to think of Gerald with anything but anger, even now when pity would have been more appropriate, because Gerald was after all the loser. ...

'I don't just mean now and then,' said Amanda.

'No? Well, what do you mean?'

'Why does anything have to change?'

'Why?' He looked at her clear thoughtful face and was silent. She seemed all at once to have removed herself so far from him that he had no hope of finding words that could survive the journey between them. 'How can you say that? Everything's changed.'

'No.'

'So we go back and it's all like it was.'

'Not just like, but –'

'You and Gerald can carry on, open your shop, is that it? What am I supposed to do?'

'I don't know.'

'You don't know. That's great, that's really. …' he paused, made incoherent by anger and dismay. 'I don't ever want to see Gerald again. I thought you'd understand that.'

'I do understand. I don't see why it should make any difference to me, that's all.'

'Oh, Christ, Amanda!' he said helplessly.

'He hasn't got anyone else.'

'Nor have I.'

'I know,' she said, in a tone that he, sensitive beyond bearing, found altogether too casual. 'But Gerald –'

'Are you sure,' he broke in, bitterly, 'that it's really me you want?'

'I don't have to decide between you.'

'If I said you did?'

'You haven't the right.'

'Haven't I, though?'

'No,' she said calmly. A sense of certitude had grown in her while she slept, and opened out into full flower in the first minutes of early morning, that she could control the pattern of their lives, by giving to Denny and to Gerald as much as she chose to give, no more; if she stood firm now, everything must resolve itself into order around her.

Denny hesitated, half-wanting still to take the chance of forcing her into choice, but the consequences to him seemed suddenly so terrifying that he drew back. 'All right,' he said. 'You know you've got me, anyway. Whatever happens. I'll try. … But,' he could not resist adding, 'Gerald may not want to see you again, not if you're with me. Had you thought of that?'

'That's up to him. Isn't it?' she said.

'For a start, he won't believe you didn't tell me where you

were. He'll think we planned this.'

'Maybe he will.'

'So?'

'We'll have to see, that's all.' She looked quickly round the room. 'Shall we go?'

'If you're ready.'

'Yes.'

Outside, mist wrapped the hills. There was no sky, no distance; everything was grey and soundless. Their feet left dark tracks in the dew-silvered grass. Even by the time they had reached the garage at the side of the road, the outlines of the house had already become blurred. 'Is there anyone out there at all, I wonder?' Denny said.

'I expect so,' said Amanda, seriously, as though there were indeed a possibility that the rest of the world had vanished overnight.

'Do you want me to drive?'

She shook her head. 'Later, maybe.'

'You're tired.'

'So are you. I'll be all right. And it's easier for me, I know the road.'

In the car, she turned to him. 'Everything will be all right.'

He caught the slight upward inflection of her voice. 'Are you asking me or telling me?'

'I don't know. Both.'

'Yes,' he said, 'yes, it will.'

36

Gerald expected all day that Denny would return at any moment. When it grew late and there was still no sign of him, he began to feel uneasy. It was not that he cared what had become of him, only, it was too much to hope that he had gone for good, and so he would be back and there would be scenes, there couldn't help being. The night before he'd thought, almost, that he had settled Denny; now he felt less sure. Would Denny feel that he'd been settled? Unlikely. He'd go on trying to see Amanda, and sooner or later, Gerald knew, he'd succeed. There wasn't any way of preventing it that he could see, and he was not as confident as he had been that Amanda would refuse to listen to Denny. He realised that he hadn't, actually, the slightest idea of what she felt about Denny. It hadn't occurred to him to ask; he had been concerned only with separating them. It had seemed enough at the time. Now that he was alone, and unable to influence in any way what either of them did or thought, he knew that it wasn't enough. Nothing like it. Amanda's need for solitude took on a sinister aspect. What did she have to think about?

He could not sleep. It was intolerable to be doing nothing, even if there was nothing that could be done. He took pen and paper and began to write to Amanda. It was not easy: no sooner had he started than he was seized by the conviction that the only thing to do was to admit that he had not told her the truth. He wrote, and scribbled out what he had written, wrote again, and tore the page; finally he pushed the unwritten letter aside. Whatever he had to say to her must wait until she was with him and he could choose his words to suit her reactions. *As long as I see her again before he does*, he thought. He sat a little longer, with his weary mind turning over again and again what needed to be said and done, and leaned his head on his arms and slept at the table, waking to find the electric light dim against the light of morning. He was still alone in the house.

As this second day wore on, he wondered more and more at Denny's continued absence, until a thought occurred to him that not only explained it, but also encouraged him to hope that things might after all turn out easier than he had feared. Wasn't it at least possible, he asked himself, that Denny had simply given up? *Are they ever really cured, isn't it always there, the craving*? He remembered his mother, the times when she had seemed, almost, to manipulate circumstances so that they gave her an excuse for drinking. Six months off it once, full of self-congratulation and bright plans for the future, but the submerged need nudging her into a situation where she could throw off pretence, turn back with what had seemed to Gerald to be relief. He found that he was wishing hard that something of the sort had happened to Denny. It would make things a lot simpler, and be no one's fault, only Denny's. ... He was glad now, that he hadn't managed to write that letter to Amanda. There might never be any need to tell her that he'd lied.

By evening, he was sure that he was right. He locked and bolted all the doors so that if Denny should after all return he could not be surprised by him (because if he had got hold of something there wasn't any knowing what he might do). It worried him that Amanda had not rung that day. She'd promised. ... He made himself stay awake as long as he could, but tiredness overwhelmed him, and at last he went to bed. The telephone dragged him out of his first sleep, and he staggered down the stairs. It was a wrong number. After that he slept only fitfully, fears darting quick and sudden as silverfish across his mind. In the morning he tried to reach her at the cottage although he had promised that he would not, but the number was unlisted.

There was nothing, then, that he could do, nothing in that direction, at least. There were any number of things that had to be done, he supposed, in the shop, in the yard; there was a whole heap of stuff in the shed, waiting to be sorted. He felt no enthusiasm for work, but he knew that it would be better to be doing something, anything, rather than sit alone with his thoughts. He left the shop door locked and taped a notice to the window asking callers to come round by the yard entrance. Perhaps when Amanda came back from Wales he'd ask her to help out in the shop. He could do with someone; after all, Denny wasn't going to be around. ... He should have done it before, he should have kept her near him all the time, not left her on her own so that Denny could sneak in. ... Nothing might have happened then, or if it had he could have seen what was going on in time to do something about it. ... What had she wanted with Denny? What had he meant to her, how had he persuaded her. ... His brain crawled with memories. Amanda's shining hair eclipsed as she and Denny held each other, unaware of the watcher across the street. The pressure of her mouth. … *It isn't necessary, all that,* he told her silently. *It's nothing. It's only Denny made you think that's what you wanted. We'd have been all right, were, can be … it isn't love, you know, not that. Love's something quite different.* …

He did not notice that anyone had entered the yard until he heard his name spoken. When he looked up, and recognised his callers as policemen, his first thought was, *so I was right about Denny, no real cure, the least strain cracks them and they're back where they were*; and then, hard on the heels of this, trampling the jubilation he felt at the idea that Denny had so neatly disposed of himself, came the thought, *or is it about that dish? I might have known there'd be trouble … his fault again, always his*; but one of the policemen was speaking and not about the dish, not about Denny, it was Amanda's name that Gerald heard, and he could not see why they should be talking about her.

'I'm sorry,' he said, 'I didn't –'

The policeman was saying something about an accident. Gerald felt as though his ears were blocked. The voice seemed to be coming from a long way off. What it said made no sense at all. 'I don't understand,' he said. 'She's all right?' He saw the two men exchange glances, and no expression in the eyes of the one speaking to him, repeating, it was clear from his elaborately patient tone, something that had already been said.

'Car?' said Gerald. 'She isn't here, you know. She's in Wales.'

'Yes. That was where the accident took place.'

Oh no, said Gerald, he did not think, to anyone but himself, *there has to be some mistake here*. He shook his head as though he were trying to free it from the words that had erroneously wandered into it. He must, after all, have spoken aloud, because the policeman said, 'No mistake, I'm afraid.'

Gerald did not think there was anything he could say, or wanted to say even. He began to move slowly towards the house. His feet felt in an odd way detached from him; he had to think quite hard about what he was doing to get them to move at all. Most peculiar. … The voice, following him, held him in his tracks. This time it was asking about Denny. He couldn't make out why. 'Well, I don't know where he is, do I,' he said.

'Works here, doesn't he?'

'Yes,' said Gerald. 'No, he doesn't, not any more. He isn't here. Anyway it isn't anything to do with him, you know.'

'Sorry?'

'I don't know what you want to ask about him for.'

'Routine. – So you've no idea where he might be?'

Gerald shook his head. There were still things lodged inside it that made it difficult to think. 'It doesn't matter anyway, does it?'

'You'll be here, will you, if we need to ask you anything more?'

'I suppose so,' said Gerald. They turned to go, and he said, 'Look, I'm still not clear, could you tell me …' and waited, though he wasn't really sure what he was waiting for.

'What is it you're not clear about?'

'What happened.'

'Well, it's hard to say at this stage. There being no witnesses.'

'Witnesses?'

'There seems to have been no other vehicle involved.'

'I see,' said Gerald, seeing nothing. 'When?'

'Yesterday morning.'

Yesterday, thought Gerald. *No, that really isn't possible. She can't have been dead ever since yesterday because I've been thinking about her all this time, and I'd have known … I was just talking to her, wasn't I, just now, before they came, and I couldn't have done that if it was true, what they said.* … Although he couldn't remember them doing so, they must have said goodbye and gone out of the yard, because he was alone now. He went indoors, walked through to the shop, and took down the notice from the door. *Not open today*, he said to himself. He went back into the yard and shut, but did not bolt, the gate. *In case Denny comes back*. It didn't seem to matter very much any more, the things Denny had done and said. Gerald just wished he'd return from wherever it was he'd gone, because he didn't think he could bear to be alone much longer.

Noises came from the street but Gerald was hardly aware of them. The silence of the house was what sounded loudest in his ears. He sat for a long time at the table in the kitchen, staring at nothing. One of the taps was dripping. He watched the bead of water gather, elongate and fall, and heard the soft splatter as it hit the sink, and no sooner had it vanished than another started to swell from the tap. He watched the drops, a hundred or more, as though they were the most important things in the world. He had to force himself, finally, to turn his head away. By then the sound of it had grown so loud that he did not want to stay in the same room. He went upstairs, not to his own room, but to Denny's. He had no idea why. In all the time that Denny had been living here, Gerald had been in his room only once. He had been woken in the night by screams and had hurried to see what was the matter. Denny was kicking and twisting violently and Gerald had been greatly alarmed because he thought that Denny must be having some kind of fit and he did not know what he ought to do about it. But Denny had all at once slipped out of the grasp of his nightmare and had been furious to find Gerald standing there, a witness to his unconscious terror. Gerald went back to his own room, feeling embarrassed, and, somehow, hurt. After that Denny had started to talk to him, to tell him things, but Gerald sometimes had the impression that what he was really saying was, *how about this then, since you're curious?* and this saddened him, because he really didn't want to know the things Denny told him, any more than he had wanted to know those that his mother had occasionally flung at him.

It was a kind of curiosity now, though, that took him to Denny's room. He thought he might find something of Amanda there, who knows what, a letter, perhaps, had they been writing to each other, notes slipped from hand to hand when he was not looking? Something, anything, to revive his anger, which would be more bearable than this numbed unreality. He found the things you find in other people's rooms, especially when you are there without their knowledge. Drifts of soft grey fluff in the corners, crumpled socks, hairs trailing from a comb. No letters, nothing at all revelatory, except, maybe, for a couple of magazines, run-of-the-mill stuff, corner-shop porn, but Gerald was disgusted: *that, and her*. ...

The Book of Changes lay face-down, broken-backed on the floor where Denny had slung it. Mechanically Gerald picked it up, smoothing the creased pages, and then reached for the other book that lay open on the bed. It was only when he had it in his hands that he realised it was an atlas, and that it was open at the map of Wales. At first it seemed to him no more than a sick coincidence. He stared at it, seeking and eventually finding among the unfamiliar names the one that was fixed on his mind. He crushed the book against his body as though by doing so he could obliterate the place and what had happened there. It was only gradually that he began to ask himself why Denny had been looking at that particular page. The answer was there almost before the question had fully formed itself in his mind, and other questions were scurrying about like beetles under a lifted stone. How had Denny known? Had she told him? Had she expected him? There was all of a sudden too much to think about; he could not cope with any of it. His conscious mind had almost ceased to function by the time that he was in the van driving away.

37

The journey took far longer than he would have thought, if he had been able to think about such a thing; so much longer that he was forced at last to pull in by the roadside and rest. Behind his closed lids his eyes burned with the remembered glare of approaching headlamps, and in spite of his exhaustion he did not expect to sleep, only to recover a little; but he did fall asleep, almost immediately, and slept surprisingly well. In the morning – for it was morning when he woke up: the sky was streaked with red like tongues of flame – he felt much clearer in his mind and was able to consider what he ought to do.

In the town, he went to the police station and asked about the accident. He thought it would be a simple business, but it was not. Instead of being given the information he wanted, he was told to wait, for far longer than could possibly have been necessary. And when at last someone came to talk to him, it was to ask and not to answer questions. He couldn't see the point of them; he felt himself growing confused again. He said, interrupting, 'I just wanted to see her, that's all.'

'I don't think that would be of any use.'

'It can't be her.'

'There isn't any doubt.'

'But I've come all this way –'

'There was no need for you to do that.'

'I had to.'

'Why? Weren't you asked to stay where you were, just in case?'

'I don't know. Maybe.'

'This has been a shock for you, I'm afraid.'

'Yes. Yes, it has. ...'

And that was over, and he still knew nothing, nothing at all, and maybe would never know anything, because there was no one to ask, no one to help him, and in any case, what help could there be, what answers?

38

The road climbed steeply, a narrow grey scar on the side of a grey green hill, green with the grass that the wind, as much as the mountain sheep, kept close-bitten, grey with the rocks that jutted out from its gaunt flanks. Gerald kept the van going steadily, his eyes flickering between the road ahead and its edge where the ground fell away, now sloping, now steeply, to the valley. Beyond the valley more hills rose up to the sky, touching clouds that hung swollen with rain. The dots of grey that moved were sheep; the ones that didn't were stones. He had the window open for a clearer view. The air was moist. His eyes ached. There was a dryness behind his eyelids that hurt whenever his glance shifted.

Up ahead, where the road made yet another sharp turn, he

saw a white post that leaned at an angle. He slowed the van almost to walking pace and when he reached the corner, he stopped. He put his head out of the window and looked at the rim of the road where the grass and the earth were marked by the tracks of tyres. He did not feel like looking any further. After a little he started the van again and drove on.

The road began to drop now; the view was lost between the hills. It was not long before he came to a house. He sat for a moment looking at it, and then, because he had come this far, though he expected nothing and indeed did not know what there could be to expect, he got out and went to the door. He rang and knocked, and listened to the sounds being swallowed up by emptiness. He walked round, looking in at the windows, but the inside of the house, on this dull drear day, was too dark for him to be able to make out anything. He wondered why he had come here. He got into the van and drove slowly back the way that he had come. Just past the corner with the tilted post, he parked in a passing place and walked to the edge of the road.

The drop here was almost sheer, but further on he found a place where it was possible to get down, and he slithered on rough grass and scree, moving sideways as well as downwards, keeping a check on his position by looking back, from time to time, at the white post. Presently he saw, on the ground in front of him, marks where something heavy had struck, slid, rebounded and struck again further down. Where the ground levelled out there were fragments of broken glass and an expanse of charred blackened grass. Nothing more.

His legs shook; a cold numbing mist filled his mind. He sat down, dropping his head to his knees. The horror of Amanda's death swooped down and enfolded him. He felt, as though they had remained here in wait for him, her fear and pain; they beat on him until he screamed for them to stop, and, startled by the sound, he lifted his head to stare about him, seeing nothing but the hills and the descending clouds. Nothing moved; no one heard him. At last he got to his feet, and, as though escape were possible, began to walk away, stumbling on the rough ground, his feet heavy as stones. On the crest of a hill he slipped and fell, saving himself from falling further by clutching at tufts of grass. He inched his way cautiously downwards, not daring to stand upright. He was in a small narrow ravine, overhung with boulders, as though the stones beneath the surface had swelled and split the earth. Loose stones filled the bottom of it, sliding and crunching under his feet. He was still dazed by his near-fall and it was some time before he could stand and look further than the ground immediately in front of him.

A little way along the cleft lay something that was not the grey and green of stone and grass. He did not immediately recognise it as a human figure; only after he had stared at it for several seconds did he begin to make sense of the shape. He went closer. It was Denny, lying face down among the stones. He thought that he ought to be surprised but could not feel anything of the sort. He sat down a few feet away from the body and looked at it with a blank detached curiosity. There was little enough to see. Denny's face was half-hidden by blood and dirt and hair stiff and caked with both.

Gerald was glad, at first. He thought that now he would not ever have to see Denny again or speak to him. 'It serves you right,' he said aloud. 'You should have left her alone. We were all right.' Tears began to trickle down his face. 'You didn't have to,' he said. 'She wouldn't even have come here if it hadn't been for you. Everything would have been all right. This wouldn't have happened. It's your fault, all of it.' As he spoke he scraped up handfuls of stones and threw them in Denny's direction. His sight was blurred and his aim unsteady; few of them struck, but the action of throwing them made him feel, not better, nothing could do that, but more secure in his anger. He wished that Denny could know how he felt; the sight of him lying lifeless there no longer pleased him. It was one more betrayal; he had been utterly abandoned. *He's got off lightly*, Gerald thought. *It's nothing, death is nothing, nothing at all, compared to what it's like having to go on.* ... 'I hope it hurt, anyway,' he said. 'I hope it hurt like hell,' knowing that the words were as useless as the stones. He leaned back against the hard cold rock and stared up at the heavy sky.

He heard a noise; he could not tell what it was nor where it came from. He looked around: there was no one, nothing, not even a bird passing overhead to break the stillness with the beating of its wings; but as he lowered his glance he saw, or thought he saw, the fingers of Denny's outstretched hand move. He held his breath, thinking that he must have been mistaken; but after a minute or two they moved again, almost imperceptibly, but enough for there to be no doubt.

Gerald crouched beside Denny and listened to the sound of his breathing, which now seemed so loud and harsh that he wondered why he had not heard it from the start. He tugged at Denny's shoulder and managed to turn his inert body over; the movement forced sounds from his mouth but his eyes remained shut. 'Well,' said Gerald, letting him go. Sitting back on his heels, he watched for some reaction to his presence; none came. 'Can you hear me?' he asked. 'Are you listening?' Denny's silence seemed to him wilful. 'You'd better,' he said. 'You'd better listen. You'd better say something.' He reached out and pulled Denny part upright; his head rolled back heavily. 'What were you doing here? What happened?' He began to shake him; at each jolt Denny's eyes were jerked open a little, showing whitely, with nothing looking out of them. 'You could tell me at least,' said Gerald. Denny was making noises with no meaning to them. Gerald let him slump back on the ground. 'No one's going to find you here, you know,' he said, conversationally. 'No one's going to look for you. They don't know you're here.'

He got to his feet and looked among the fallen stones until he found one that seemed suitable. He picked it up and hefted it in his hands, feeling its weight and the sharp edges. He stood beside Denny and held the stone high. 'Can you hear?' he asked, looking down between his upstretched arms. 'Can you see?' But there was no movement now from Denny, and no sound. Slowly, Gerald lowered the stone, and when it was at waist height he slung it harmlessly a few feet away. It thumped against a patch of bare earth, bounced and landed rattling among other stones.

Gerald began to walk, following the ravine downhill until the steep sides flattened out and became climbable. He talked to himself as he walked. 'After all,' he said, 'it's better really if he just stays there. He shouldn't have come.' His words slipped into the rhythm of his steps. 'Nothing to do with me ... and no one knows ... he can lie there and rot ... serves him right. ...' Gradually what he was saying lost all sense and degenerated into a slurred repetitive babble.

He headed towards the place where he had left the van. While he was still some way from the road, the clouds opened up, suddenly, as though their dragging bellies had been ripped apart by the hills; the rain started falling, thick as entrails, but cold. Gerald gasped with the shock and tried to run, but it wasn't ground for running on. A fierce wind followed the rain, hurling it slantwise at him. By the time he reached the van he was exhausted and chilled to the bone. He huddled in his seat and listened to the thudding of the rain on the roof, growing softer till the sound was no more than the light tapping of fingers, and then in an instant gathering strength and slamming down on the metal, so that Gerald thought that it might force its way through. He could see very little beyond the rivulets that poured across the windows. As he sat there, feeling water from his soaked hair trickling down his back, the memory of what had just occurred hit him as suddenly and as violently as the rain had done. It was like recalling a dream that had been lost on waking; only, this dream had a life of its own and went on although he was no longer the dreamer. He saw himself and the raised stone; for a moment he saw blood and shattered bone and spilt brains, but then that picture dissolved into streaming rain that washed the blood from Denny's upturned face and poured into his nostrils and his mouth, filling his lungs, drowning. Gerald's anger fell from him like a shrivelled husk, useless. He leaped from the van and hurtled recklessly downhill, charging the rain with his bent head like a battering ram. He ran too fast to fall; his feet did not touch the ground long enough to stumble. A few yards from the edge of the ravine he managed to check his pace, and came muddily to a standstill.

He could see the scattered stones and Denny's dark shape. He was moving; slowly, awkwardly, but moving, like a seal, using his elbows to drag his weight along, inch by inch. Gerald yelled at him, but if he heard he gave no sign of it. Gerald scrambled down the slope and ran across the ankle-twisting stones. Before he reached him, the impulse that had briefly powered Denny had died, and he lay flat and motionless as he had been when Gerald had first seen him.

Gerald knelt beside him and touched him, gently, brushing the hair back from his face. Denny gave no sign of life. The rain continued to fall, steadily. Gerald reached for his wrist and held it but could not tell whether the pulse that he felt beating was Denny's or his own. He leaned closer and caught a faint intermittent warmth that told him Denny was still breathing. He took off his coat and with it he covered Denny as best he could. It was not much use: the rain had already begun to soak through to the lining, but the gesture comforted Gerald, at least. For a moment he thought of attempting to carry Denny up the hill. He would have been glad to but was afraid of the damage that this might cause. 'I'll get someone,' he said. 'An ambulance. That's what we need, isn't it?' He hardly thought that Denny would hear, but, just in case: 'I'm sorry,' he said. 'What I said before ... what I did. I didn't mean it.' He got to his feet. 'Don't move, will you. I won't be long.'

It was strange, but as he hurried back up the hill he was aware of a feeling that was almost like happiness.

39

Perhaps it was the rain falling icily that brought Denny back to consciousness. There had been moments, while he was lying there, when he had climbed briefly out of blackness, but never long enough for him to do more than recognise pain, to fumble in his mind for memories of what had happened, before sliding back into the pit. This time it was different. It was not a gradual hazy awakening; it was sudden and alarming. He could not breathe. He choked and coughed and turned his head, and water ran out of his mouth and nose. Someone was throwing things at him. His body ached, he was being pelted, all the time, he could not tell with what. He wanted to draw himself up close but his legs would not do as he asked, and all movement hurt. He tried to raise his head a little to see what was going on. He vaguely thought that his attacker must be Gerald, though he didn't know why he should think that. He saw stones, and rain bouncing off them, forming rivulets on the ground, and then he realised that he had no human assailant. He let his head fall again, burying it in the crook of his arm.

He remembered now driving with Amanda through the mist. He had been tired and had closed his eyes, and she had been speaking, though what she had been saying he could not now recall; and then, in some order that wasn't clear to him yet, had come a swerve, a drop, metallic crashing, a hopeless and terrified cry. The world spun, cold air was all around him, and sharp edges; the breath was knocked out of his lungs, his hands reached out and closed on nothing, and the nothing hurt. Far away, but inside his head at the same time, and deafening, there was a booming noise and then no noise at all.

As soon as he had grasped where he was and how he had got there, he knew that he must find Amanda. No one else had; they would have found him too. He raised himself on his elbows and discovered that, if he moved them forward, the rest of his body followed. Simple. The only thing was it hurt so much; but when he stopped the pain didn't, so he thought he might as well keep on. Even when he lifted his head, and the effort of that was too great to do it very often or for very long, he could see nothing but grey rocks and the rain that fell endlessly. His breath came in sobs that seemed to split his chest apart. He thought his body might at any moment be shattered into pieces by the strain of movement, but pain knotted itself around him and held him together.

After he could not tell how long he grew aware of a new noise above the drumming of the rain and the slithering scraping sound of his own progress, but his brain refused to concern itself with anything but the task of moving him forwards, although by now all effort was largely wasted. He rested his head on rough stone and felt the ground shudder beneath him. He knew now, dimly, that it was footsteps that he was hearing, but he had no longer the energy to be curious or glad. Somewhere, on the other side of thick darkness, was a voice, and something touched him, but he was floating now, and beyond reach. It could in any case have been a dream; there was not much of reality about it. Later though there were more voices, and movement. He was being torn apart, he was being enveloped. Once, he opened his eyes, and saw, or thought he saw, Gerald, and wondered what Gerald was doing to him, and why; and then he knew he must be dreaming, because how could Gerald be there, and anyway when he looked again there were only lights, dazzling after all that grey, and then his arm was gripped tightly and he felt a needle slide in, and after that there was nothing at all.

40

Gerald sat on a bench in a long white corridor. Occasionally people in white coats, carrying piles of buff folders, walked past, or nurses whose aprons rustled dryly like the sound of wind sifting through dead leaves, or patients in slippers, shuffling and flapping, and none of them did more than turn their heads briefly in his direction as they passed. He had been sitting there for so long that he had become as unremarkable as the bench on which he sat or the notice forbidding smoking taped to the wall opposite. The air was warm and used, heavy with the smell of antiseptic and polish and thin metallic soup. The sky was darkening outside the uncurtained windows. It was now nearly twenty-four hours since Denny had been brought here and Gerald did not know what was happening and no longer dared to ask, since those whom he had already asked either had not known or had been too concerned with other things to answer with more than vague platitudinous phrases.

From time to time Gerald got up and bought himself a cup of

tea from the canteen, or went to the lavatory, or simply walked a little in the corridor. His feet felt heavy, as though he were walking through water. He thought he should be hungry: he could not remember when he had last eaten; but the biscuits that he bought were dry and tasteless in his mouth like sawdust and he did not manage to finish more than one of them. He tipped his head back against the wall, closing his eyes, wishing he could sleep. He had tried to sleep in the van the night before, without much success. Perhaps it would have been better if he had found somewhere more comfortable, but he doubted it. There was a kind of buzzing in his ears that would not go away, but rather increased, when he shook his head to dislodge it. He thought it would have kept him awake wherever he was.

It was terrible, how his mind turned to Amanda, however hard he tried to shut her out. She was everywhere, seeping like smoke through the least crack, swelling in his thoughts until he feared his memory would not be able to bear it any longer, would split and lose its contents, and she be dispersed and drift away, floating fragments, beyond recall. He concentrated on irrelevant things, the biscuit crumbs that his restless fingers were rubbing to fine dust in his pocket, the draught that fluttered the edge of the poster on the wall whenever a certain door was opened, anything, so long as he could keep his memory intact.

He wished that they would let him see Denny, speak to him. He had never in his life felt such a need to talk to someone, not for comfort, since there could be no comfort, but only so that his thoughts might not be lost forever in a void of meaninglessness. *He'll help, he must, or else I might as well have left him after all. To keep her real for me. That's what she wanted.* And it did indeed seem to him now that he had heard Amanda's voice in the rain and the wind on the mountainside.

41

There was a voice somewhere near Denny, a voice with no face, asking questions. He wanted it to stop. Thinking hurt too much, it was a physical pain, as bad as if his battered body were being forced to hold itself upright. He turned his head to one side, away from the voice. It made no difference.

'I don't know,' he said. 'I don't know what happened.'

Try to think.

'Doesn't matter.'

You might find you remembered something … could help. …

'Help?' Denny thought about this. He could make no sense of it. His mind was strewn with disconnected images, tattered and frayed about the edges. There was something that puzzled him. 'Gerald,' he said.

Yes? What about him?

'I don't know. He was there.'

Where was that, then?

'Wasn't he?'

Tell us about Gerald.

'He was throwing things at me.'

Things?

'No. That's wrong. I think. It was raining, that's what. The rain was hard. Like stones.'

And Gerald?

'That was later. I think it was.'

And before? Can you remember what happened before?

'Before?'

The voice prompted: *You were in the car. …*

'The car, oh yes. …' Memory punched his mind, a hard and sudden blow. 'Where's Amanda?'

Don't worry.

'Is she all right? What –'

Think about the car. Just for the moment. Think. …

He thought about it. He remembered how the windows had misted with their breath, almost immediately, and how the mist outside had clung around the car. But Amanda knew the road, he remembered her saying that. Perhaps the mist had confused her and made the road unfamiliar, perhaps … or perhaps it was the brakes, because she did say, didn't she, that there was something wrong, but Gerald. … It occurred to him that he ought to be saying these things aloud, as he had been asked to, and with an effort, he found speech. 'Fixed the brakes.'

Who fixed the brakes?

'Well, Gerald, of course. I said, didn't I?'

How do you know?

'I suppose he did. She said there was something wrong.'

When did she say that? Can you remember exactly?

'I meant to check but I forgot. … I should've, shouldn't I? Gerald mucking about with it. …'

Did you see him?

'I thought I did, but. … Anyway, he's in London. We were going back, she said. … He won't like it.'

Gerald? What won't he like?

'Well … me and her.'

You and her?

'You know. …' Pain was beginning to worm its way through him once more, sucking juices from his brain. 'He wanted. …'

What did he want?

'Where is she?'

Can you just tell us –

'Where's Amanda?'

About Gerald, can you tell us –

'Where –' Things hurt enough already without the icicle fear stabbing his heart. '– is she, where –' He began to scream, although each breath he drew seemed to tear at his lungs like claws. The voice left off, and then there were other voices, and then the needle in his arm that put an end to questions.

42

It was now quite dark outside. The hospital corridor remained bright but there was less movement in it. No one was here now who did not have to be, and a stillness had fallen, gradually, as though somewhere, one by one, switches had been thrown. Gerald wondered whether soon someone would come to tell him that he had to go. He did not feel he had enough energy left in him to move; it had drained out of him during his long hours of waiting.

It was not a nurse or a doctor, no one to do with the hospital at all. It was a policeman. Gerald did as he was told, like an automaton. Nothing made sense in the least; it did not occur to him though to ask questions. Only, as they left the womb-like warmth of the hospital, and the sharp moist night-air stung his face, he woke enough from his trance to say, 'But can't I see him, before ... I was waiting. ...' No one replied, and then he thought that Denny must have died, in spite of all he had done to save him; he wanted to ask, but was afraid that putting it into words would make it true, so he remained silent until he was once again in light and warmth, and other people began to do the asking. It was some time before he realised what their questions meant, why he had been brought here, and then he could only shake his head, bewildered. 'But I wouldn't have hurt her,' he said, over and over again; and finally they took pity on him, or grew tired of him, he couldn't tell which, and let him sleep.

43

'Sorry about that,' said Denny.

Everything was white: walls, sheets, blankets. Denny himself seemed unnaturally clean, as though a layer of skin had been peeled from him to reveal a new, unused one. Gerald thought, looking at his hands lying against his sides on the sharp-creased, tightly-tucked bedcover, that this was the first time he'd ever seen Denny's fingernails without a crescent of dirt at the ends.

'It's all right,' said Gerald.

'Of course I didn't know what I was saying half the time.'

'Yes, I know.'

'The thing was,' Denny went on, 'they didn't think I'd make it. They wanted to get something while they still had the chance, I suppose.'

'It's all right,' Gerald said again.

'They tell me I'm very lucky to have got through,' said Denny, 'so I suppose I am.' There was a note in his voice that suggested otherwise.

'When I found you,' said Gerald, 'I thought at first. ...'

'Yes, I expect you did.' Denny looked at Gerald, thoughtfully. 'I should thank you or something.'

'Oh well.'

'Though I don't know why you bothered.'

'You'll be all right,' said Gerald.

'That isn't really what I meant, but ... forget it. Yes. So they keep telling me.'

'They can do all sorts of things these days, can't they.'

'Oh yes,' said Denny. 'Good as new.' He looked at the lines of strain round Gerald's eyes and mouth. His face seemed somehow to have shrunken, caved in. It was as though there was something eating away at it from the inside. 'You look rough,' he said. 'They give you a bad time?'

'What?' said Gerald.

'The fuzz. Did they?'

'Not really, no. They were all right. But ...' he rubbed his hand briefly across his eyes, which were aching, as they always did, 'a bad time, yes. ...'

Amanda's ghost hung in the sterile air between them, and each was reluctant to call attention to it. Denny's unnaturally clean fingernails teased a loose thread from the bedspread. Finally Gerald said – the words pumped out of him as though he had nothing to do with it – 'I think about her all the time you know.'

There wasn't anything Denny could think of to say in reply to this. He had thought about Amanda often, yes, of course, but not under compulsion. And when he did think of her, it was to find his feelings numbed. He probed deeper and deeper into his memories, expecting pain each minute: there was none. The closeness of his own death, during that confused shadowy period when people had been coaxing and bullying him back into life, had somehow anaesthetised his emotions, perhaps even excised them altogether. He was not sure, at this moment, who, out of himself and Gerald, was most to be pitied.

'What happened?' Gerald was asking.

'Christ, Gerald, I don't know,' Denny said wearily. 'It was all so quick, and then, I don't know, it just seems such a long time ago now. ...'

'I didn't mean that.'

'Does it really matter now?'

'Yes, it does.'

Denny thought, *I can tell him what I like, because there's no one knows except me*, and then he thought, *but it won't change anything, will it, whatever I tell him*, and he said, 'Nothing happened.' It seemed to him to be the truth, now, as he said it.

'Nothing?'

'Not a lot. We were coming back. She wanted. ...'

'What?'

'To see you.'

'Why?'

'Just to see you. Gerald –' this all was now to him like

something that had happened elsewhere, at another time, to people that he didn't know, 'we were going to get married, but she didn't want ... she hoped you'd understand, she didn't want that to change things between you and her.'

'She said that.'

'Yes. Of course I suppose it wouldn't have worked out but. ... I did love her, Gerald. I don't know if you realised. I'd have done anything she wanted, I mean, I would have tried but. ... It's all gone, you know. There's nothing left, all that. ... You shouldn't have bothered. You'd have done better just to go away. Or finish me off. Would have been kinder, really.'

'I did think about it.'

'Which?'

'Both.'

'Did you? Well, I wish you had done. I really mean that. Either would be better than –'

'You were with her,' said Gerald. He seemed to have stopped listening to Denny. 'You saw her last.'

'Oh,' said Denny. 'That kind of thing really isn't important. Time, and all that. It only matters if you make it do.'

'Maybe,' said Gerald. 'That reminds me. I don't know why. I brought you your book.'

'You what?'

'Your book. I thought you might like to have it.' Gerald took from his pocket Denny's copy of the *I Ching* and laid it on the bed between them.

'Oh, that was nice of you,' said Denny. He did not feel he ever wanted to ask questions about anything again, but he was touched that Gerald should have thought to bring it.

'When will you get out of here?' said Gerald.

'I don't know. They haven't said. Not for a bit, I shouldn't think.'

'Listen,' said Gerald. 'Things I said. I'm sorry.'

'It's okay. I said things too. Forget it.'

'I didn't mean ...'

'None of it matters any more, anyway.'

'You're coming back, aren't you, when they do let you out.'

'I don't suppose,' said Denny, after a pause, 'I'd be all that much use. Not like this.'

'Good as new, you said.'

'I doubt it.'

'Anyway,' said Gerald, 'you'll need help, won't you. At first.'

'No thanks,' said Denny.

'I'd be glad –'

'I've had enough of being grateful to you,' said Denny. 'I don't think I can take any more, thanks all the same.'

'That isn't what I want,' said Gerald. 'Gratitude. It isn't that at all.'

'Don't worry about me,' said Denny. 'I'll be okay. – How's business, anyway?'

'Oh well,' said Gerald, 'I haven't felt much like ... well. You know.'

'Yes,' said Denny, 'yes, I can imagine.' He hesitated a moment, then, 'Still, there's all that money, isn't there? We'll both of us be all right.' He waited for some reaction from Gerald; none came. 'Christ, what a joke though,' he said.

'Joke?'

'No, not really. ... But when I heard about it, it seemed so, I don't know. ... I wish she hadn't done that. She should have left it all to you.'

'Why?'

'Oh, I don't know,' said Denny. 'Keep it in the family or something ... it really doesn't matter to me.'

'You think it matters to me?'

'You'll be glad of it sometime I expect. You can do things –'

'Not without her,' said Gerald. There was a long silence. Denny closed his eyes, as though he were hoping that when he next opened them Gerald might have vanished. Gerald said, 'You think it was my fault, don't you?'

'What?' said Denny, startled.

'What happened. You think it was my fault. You told them.'

'I never,' said Denny. 'They got it wrong. I don't know what I said. It wasn't that.'

'It was anyway,' said Gerald. 'My fault. Of course it really was.' Denny heard, or thought he heard, an odd note of triumph in Gerald's voice, as if he took some satisfaction in having the last word. 'I made her go away,' continued Gerald. 'I wanted her away from you.'

'I thought it was her idea, going off like that.'

'Only because of what I told her.'

'Yes, but then if I – oh Christ,' said Denny, suddenly revolted, 'let's not argue about whose fault it is, shall we? It's like fighting over bones.'

'At least you haven't got her, anyway.'

'As if we either of us ever did or could have,' said Denny. 'It doesn't make a lot of difference now, does it? I don't care, you know, I don't care about any of it. It's all pointless. Why don't you go away?'

Gerald did not speak. It was some time before Denny noticed that tears were slipping from his blank eyes. Gerald was sitting stiff-backed on the comfortless hospital chair and weeping in silence. His hands were clenched in his lap and made no movement to hide or wipe away the tears. Denny watched him, and briefly, as though their minds had touched, he felt Gerald's pain.

'I don't think it's doing you any good, being on your own,' he said at last. 'I think you're the one wants looking after, not me. They'll have you at the funny farm if you're not careful.' He could not tell from Gerald's expression whether or not he had heard him, but he went on, 'We could see what the *I Ching* says, I suppose. Seeing as you brought it. We might as well. Got any money?'

'What?' said Gerald. He raised his hands to his face and carefully blotted his tears.

'Three coins, all the same. Yes, those'll do. You want to ask a question?'

Gerald shook his head.

'Okay, then, I will.' Denny paused, and threw the coins, totting up the numbers between each throw.

'I don't see how that can tell you anything,' said Gerald. 'It's just chance.'

'Yes, well, it only seems that way,' said Denny. He leafed through the book. 'Chung Fu,' he said. 'That's it. Inmost

Sincerity. Sounds okay, doesn't it? *Moves even pigs and fish, and leads to good fortune*.'

'Pigs and fish?' said Gerald. 'It doesn't make sense.'

'Of course it doesn't actually mean pigs and fish,' said Denny. 'It means something else.'

'Then what's the point?'

'That is the point. What it really means is the point.'

'Why doesn't it just say what it really means?'

'Oh well,' said Denny, 'you can't expect to find answers in a book, can you?'

'Where do you find them then?'

'Well, that's the question, isn't it?'

'Where do you?'

'In yourself, where else?'

'What did you ask it, anyway?'

'Something like, how the hell I'm going to put up with you, that's what.'

'Oh,' said Gerald. 'Does it make any sense to you? The pigs and fish, and all that?'

'I'll work on it.'

'I still think it's rubbish.'

'What isn't? But we got to get through somehow. It's a place to start.'

'I think I'll go now,' said Gerald.

'Look after yourself, will you? I might just need you.'

'I'll try. – You know,' said Gerald, getting up, leaning confidently towards Denny, 'I think I hear her, sometimes. She tells me things.'

'Does she, then?'

'Is it possible, do you think?'

'How would I know?'

'Do you really think I'm going mad?'

'No, not really. Like they used to say, it's whatever turns you on. You hear voices, I do the *I Ching*. It helps to think you're not alone. Gives the whole mess some kind of meaning.'

'Yes. Well, I'll see you, then.'

'So long.'